This book belongs to:

....

....

PUFFIN BOOKS

UK | USA | Canada | Ireland | Australia
India | New Zealand | South Africa

Puffin Books is part of the Penguin Random House group of companies
whose addresses can be found at global.penguinrandomhouse.com.

www.penguin.co.uk
www.puffin.co.uk
www.ladybird.co.uk

First published 2020

001

The permissions on p.416–417 constitute an extension of this copyright page

The moral right of the contributors has been asserted

Set in Mundo Serif 11.5/20
Printed in Great Britain by Clays Ltd, Elcograf S.p.A.

A CIP catalogue record for this book is available from the British Library

ISBN: 978–0–241–43820–6

The National Literacy Trust is a registered charity no. 1116260
in England and Wales and no. SC042944 in Scotland

All correspondence to:
Puffin Books
Penguin Random House Children's
One Embassy Gardens, New Union Square,
5 Nine Elms Lane, London, SW8 5DA

The PUFFIN Book of BIG DREAMS

PUFFIN

Introduction

Puffin has been inspiring big dreams for 80 years. Since 1940, millions of children have grown up dreaming of snowmen coming to life, rivers of chocolate and Borrowers under the kitchen table. Here's how Puffin's own story began . . .

The first ever Puffin books didn't tell stories, but instead were factual books. In 1940, Allen Lane, the founder of Penguin, published the first four Puffin books aimed at children evacuated to the country because of World War Two – *War on Land* and *War at Sea* by James Holland, and *War in the Air* and *On the Farm* by James Gardner. In that same year, the first female editor for Puffin, Eleanor Graham, set out during an air raid to discuss the launch of a paperback series, Puffin Story Books. In 1941, the first fiction books for children were published, including *Worzel Gummidge* by Barbara Euphan Todd.

In the 1960s Puffin launched the Puffin Club, which promised to 'turn children into readers' and at its height had over 200,000 members. Membership included the quarterly magazine, *Puffin Post*, illustrated by Jill McDonald, a badge and a secret code. The Puffineers even raised money to buy a stretch of the Yorkshire coastline to be used as a puffin sanctuary.

Many Puffin stories have had lives beyond the page, transformed into tales told via film, theatre and even computer games. There are many classic children's films inspired by Puffin books: Roald Dahl's *Charlie and the Chocolate Factory*, Michael Ende's *The Neverending Story*, Anne Fine's *Madame Doubtfire*, Dick King-Smith's *The Sheep-Pig* and Jeff Kinney's *Diary of a Wimpy Kid*. In 2020, a reimagined film of Roald Dahl's *The Witches* will be scaring a new generation.

Over the years, Puffin has innovated with books of all shapes, sizes and subject matter. Puffin helped realize Eric Hill's vision for lift-the-flap on his Spot books and Allan and Janet Ahlberg's *The Jolly Postman* envelope design. In 1981, when the Rubik's Cube trend was at fever pitch, Puffin quickly produced *You Can Do the Cube* by schoolboy cube master, Patrick Bossert – which sold a million copies.

The little bird is recognized around the world. India, Australia, South Africa and New Zealand have published Puffin books by their own authors and illustrators. Puffin books have even travelled to outer space, when astronaut Tim Peake read *Goodnight Spaceman* by Michelle Robinson and Nick East from the International Space Station. In 2013 a crater on Mercury was named after the author of *A Wrinkle in Time*, Madeleine L'Engle.

Puffin's story is the sum of a million stories. Every year, editors at Puffin seek out new and exciting voices and worlds to spark readers' imaginations. On the following pages you'll meet a few of Puffin's new heroes, like Hetty Feather, Little Badman and Charlie McGuffin, as well as much-loved favourites like the BFG, Alfie and Stig.

This book has been created to celebrate Puffin's 80th birthday. On its pages you'll find stories, poems and illustrations from Puffin's past, present and future. There's also a sprinkling of big dreams from brilliantly inspiring leaders in their fields and children taking part in Puffin World of Stories, a project co-created with the National Literacy Trust to revitalize school reading spaces.

Some of these dreams are big, and some of them are small. Some are wild, and some are full of love, hope and kindness. There are dreams that are bold and brave, dreams that take you far, far away and dreams that bring you home to your very own bed. There's a dream for everyone in this book: a dream for today and a dream for the future.

National Literacy Trust

At Puffin, we believe that stories can inspire a child to feel that they can be, and do, anything. However, the reality is that not every child has access to books and stories.

One in 11 disadvantaged children in the UK don't own a book. And children's reading levels in England are the second most unequal in Europe, after Romania.

Lacking vital literacy skills holds a person back at every stage of their life. As a child they won't be able to succeed at school, as a young adult they will be locked out of the job market, and as a parent they won't be able to support their own child's learning.

That's why at Puffin we work closely with our friends at the National Literacy Trust, a charity that supports schools and communities across the UK to give disadvantaged children the literacy skills they need to succeed in life.

Five per cent of the RRP (recommended retail price) from this book will go towards helping the National Literacy Trust continue their life-changing work – from carrying out vital research, to delivering transformational programmes on the ground.

This includes Puffin World of Stories, a programme funded by Puffin, which aims to give primary schools the tools they need to help re-vitalize their school library as a hub of creativity and imagination, and inspire children to fall in love with reading.

Libraries are suffering from a chronic lack of investment – 53 per cent of teachers say they don't have a library in their school. Puffin World of Stories gives participating schools hundreds of brand-new free books and bespoke training for teachers to help them build a love of reading in their school.

In celebration of Puffin's 80th birthday, 80 schools nationwide are taking part in Puffin World of Stories in 2020. You can read pieces about their own big dreams written by children from participating schools throughout this book.

To find out more visit puffinworldofstories.co.uk.

Contents

DREAM Wild

DREAM *Bold*

DREAM Kind

DREAM *forever*

DREAM
Wild

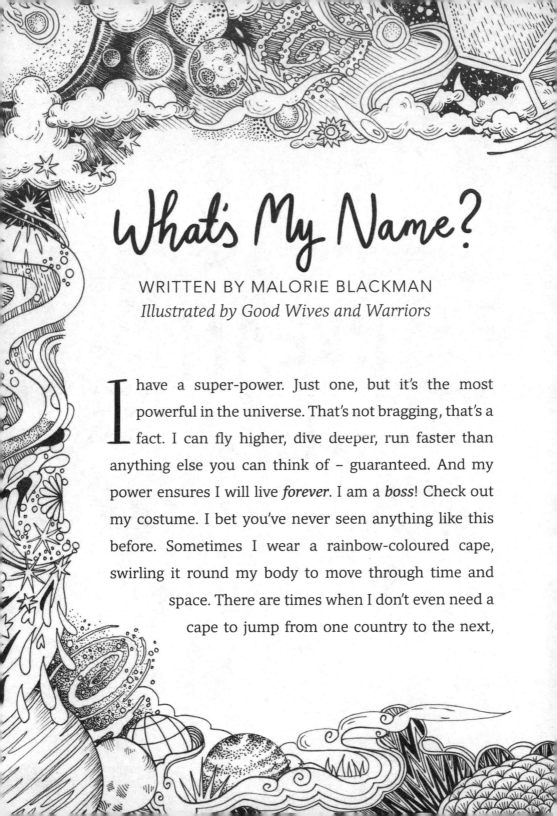

What's My Name?

WRITTEN BY MALORIE BLACKMAN

Illustrated by Good Wives and Warriors

I have a super-power. Just one, but it's the most powerful in the universe. That's not bragging, that's a fact. I can fly higher, dive deeper, run faster than anything else you can think of – guaranteed. And my power ensures I will live *forever*. I am a *boss*! Check out my costume. I bet you've never seen anything like this before. Sometimes I wear a rainbow-coloured cape, swirling it round my body to move through time and space. There are times when I don't even need a cape to jump from one country to the next,

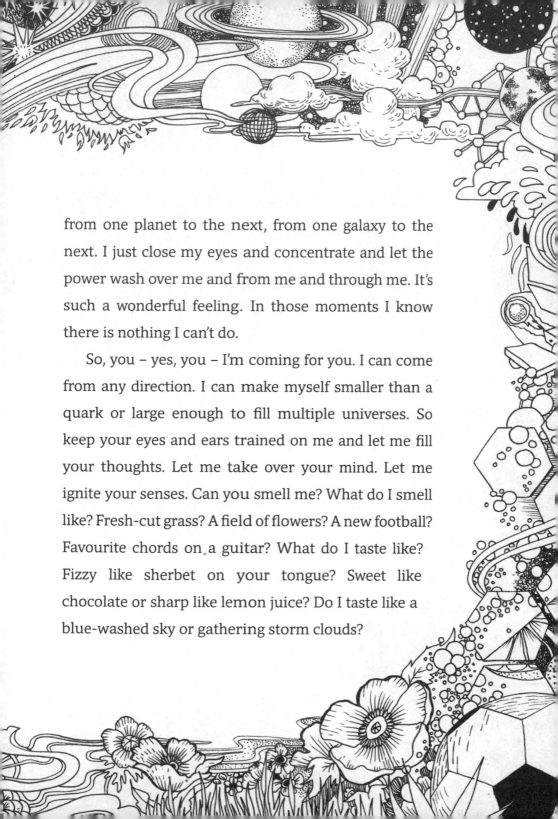

from one planet to the next, from one galaxy to the next. I just close my eyes and concentrate and let the power wash over me and from me and through me. It's such a wonderful feeling. In those moments I know there is nothing I can't do.

So, you – yes, you – I'm coming for you. I can come from any direction. I can make myself smaller than a quark or large enough to fill multiple universes. So keep your eyes and ears trained on me and let me fill your thoughts. Let me take over your mind. Let me ignite your senses. Can you smell me? What do I smell like? Fresh-cut grass? A field of flowers? A new football? Favourite chords on a guitar? What do I taste like? Fizzy like sherbet on your tongue? Sweet like chocolate or sharp like lemon juice? Do I taste like a blue-washed sky or gathering storm clouds?

Touch me. How do I feel? Get to know me, because I'm going to be with you for a long time, a lifetime – if you'll let me. I will be with you for as long as you want me. You *need* me, but if you stop feeding me, I can't grow. If you stop wanting me, I have to move on. That's just the way it is. I hope you'll always keep me in your life, because without me there would be no stories, no inventions, no games, no music, no art, no science. Without me there would be no life, no worlds. No progress. No *potential*. There would be nothing but nothingness.

Lean in closer. That's it. D'you want to hear a secret? My very biggest secret. My power only works if I share it. In fact, the more I give away, the bigger I grow and the stronger I become. That's why I'm giving it to you. And when you use this power and share it, it will grow stronger in you too. It's a lot like true love in that way – the more you give, the more you get. D'you know

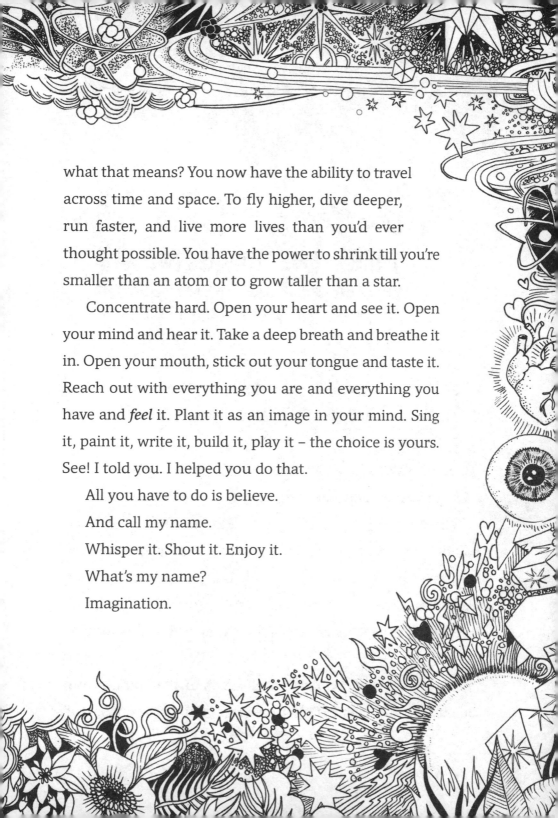

what that means? You now have the ability to travel across time and space. To fly higher, dive deeper, run faster, and live more lives than you'd ever thought possible. You have the power to shrink till you're smaller than an atom or to grow taller than a star.

Concentrate hard. Open your heart and see it. Open your mind and hear it. Take a deep breath and breathe it in. Open your mouth, stick out your tongue and taste it. Reach out with everything you are and everything you have and *feel* it. Plant it as an image in your mind. Sing it, paint it, write it, build it, play it – the choice is yours. See! I told you. I helped you do that.

All you have to do is believe.

And call my name.

Whisper it. Shout it. Enjoy it.

What's my name?

Imagination.

Pancakes AND Cha-Cha
MEET THE BIN GENIE
WRITTEN BY STUART HERITAGE
Illustrated by Nicola Slater

Two dogs sat in the park. Pancakes, the big hairy yellow one, huffed, 'I'm bored,' as he blew a tuft of fur from his eyes.

'ELEPHANTS!' shouted Cha-Cha, the little tiny brown one, as he ran round Pancakes on the grass, wagging his tail.

'Elephants?' asked Pancakes. He looked around, but he couldn't see any elephants. He could see a bench, he could see some swings, he could see a bin, but he couldn't see any elephants. 'Do you think there's an elephant in the bin?' he asked.

'I RUN AWAY!' shouted Cha-Cha, and shot off towards the bin.

Pancakes slowly pulled himself up on to all four paws and called out to his friend. 'Cha-Cha, don't jump in the bin again!'

he yelled. 'Last time you did that, you stank for a week'.

But it was too late. 'I NAUGHTY!' Cha-Cha shouted as he launched into the air, heading straight for the bin. But as he flew closer, his eyes grew bigger and bigger. 'PANCAKES!' he called out.

As Pancakes ambled up to the bin to see what the commotion was, there was a great big flash. A small purple man jumped out of the bin and on to the ground. Pancakes and Cha-Cha looked at the strange man in front of them. 'ELEPHANT?' asked Cha-Cha.

'No, little dog!' cried the man. 'I am not an elephant. I am the genie of the bin, and I am here to grant you three wishes.'

'What's a wish?' asked Pancakes, screwing up his nose.

'A wish is something that you want,' replied the Bin Genie. 'Ask me for anything and I will give it to you. I am a genie. I am magic.'

'If you're magic, why do you live in a bin?' asked Pancakes, who couldn't understand why anyone would want to live somewhere so stinky.

'Look, do you want these wishes or not?' scowled the Bin Genie.

'Sorry, yes!' replied Pancakes. 'Just let me talk to Cha-Cha first.'

Pancakes turned round and looked Cha-Cha right in the eye. 'Cha-Cha, this is very important,' he said. 'The genie says we can have anything we want. Anything at all. Do you understand?'

Cha-Cha cocked his head to one side.

'Now, I know you like elephants,' Pancakes said. 'I know elephants are all you ever talk about. But this is our big chance. We can ask for anything. What about a pizza? A pizza the size of a paddling pool! Do you want a pizza the size of a paddling pool?'

Cha-Cha cocked his head to the other side.

'OK, I'll ask him,' said Pancakes. 'Just, whatever you do, don't say "elephant".'

Pancakes turned back to the Bin Genie. 'Bin Genie, we know our first wish. Please can we have a pi–'

'ELEPHANT!' shouted Cha-Cha.

'Your wish is my command!' shouted the Bin Genie, and a giant elephant appeared in a puff of smoke.

Pancakes turned back angrily. 'Cha-Cha, what did you do? Where on earth are we going to put an elephant?'

'Sorry, Pancakes,' said Cha-Cha.

So Pancakes tried again. 'Bin Genie, our second wish is for a great big yummy, cheesy –'

'ELEPHANT!' shouted Cha-Cha.

'CHA-CHA!' screamed Pancakes.

'Your wish is my command!' shouted the genie, and a second giant elephant appeared in a puff of smoke, only this one was covered in melted cheese.

Pancakes held his paw to his face. 'Cha-Cha, what did I say?' he asked.

'No elephants,' said Cha-Cha.

'And what did you say?' asked Pancakes.

'Elephants,' said Cha-Cha.

'It's OK, I think I can fix this,' said Pancakes. He turned back to the Bin Genie. 'Bin Genie, can we start again?'

'No,' said the Bin Genie.

'So we're stuck with the elephants?' asked Pancakes.

'You have one wish left,' said the Bin Genie.

Pancakes sighed. 'I'm going to ask the Bin Genie to make the elephants go away,' he told Cha-Cha. 'That will be our last wish.'

Cha-Cha looked at Pancakes. Then he looked over at the elephants, who were happily slapping each other with their trunks. Then he looked back at Pancakes with tears in his eyes.

'No elephants go away,' Cha-Cha said quietly.

'What is your final wish?' asked the Bin Genie.

Pancakes looked at Cha-Cha. He saw how happy the elephants made him. He sighed.

'Two saddles please.'

And they rode the elephants home.

'Why do I have to sit on the cheesy one?' asked Pancakes, screwing up his nose.

ROWLEY JEFFERSON'S BIG DREAM

WRITTEN AND ILLUSTRATED BY

Jeff Kinney

My big dream, when I grow up, is to open a cupcake
shop with my mom and dad. That way we could be with
each other all day and at night, too. We could live in an
apartment above the shop and we could have a spiral slide
from our floor to the shop, so it would be easy to get to work.
And that would be good for the environment because we
wouldn't need a car. We could always tell our customers to
"have a sweet day" because that would make people smile.
Our cupcakes wouldn't have soya because I'm allergic and it
gives me hives. Sometimes, if me and my mom and dad were in a
silly mood and there were no customers in the shop, we'd put on
some Oldies music and we'd have an icing fight. But if my dad
said, "OK, that's enough fun, let's get back to work," I'd say,
"OK, but work is fun too Dad." Then he'd smile and say,
"You make me proud Rowley." And when my mom would put
me to bed at night, she'd say, "Hope you have sweet dreams,"
and I'd giggle because I'd know it was a cupcake joke.

Giant Hunters

WRITTEN BY PATRICIA FORDE

Illustrated by Rachael Saunders

The giant wakes
He creeps over the roof of our house
He fills his lungs and blows

He blows so hard
That the trees buckle in front of him
Their faces almost touching the ground
He frees his voice and roars
A booming ring
That hits the hills

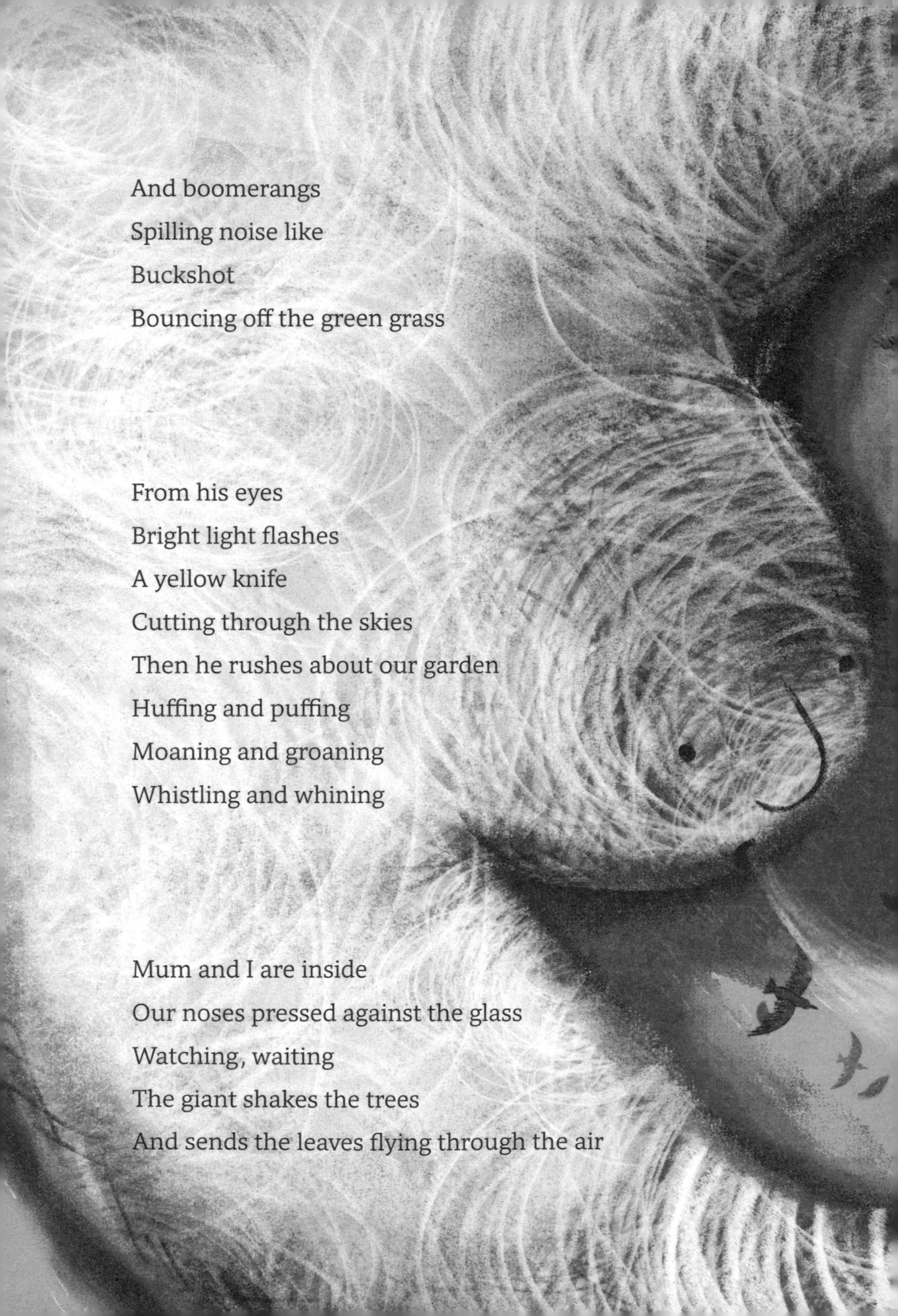

And boomerangs
Spilling noise like
Buckshot
Bouncing off the green grass

From his eyes
Bright light flashes
A yellow knife
Cutting through the skies
Then he rushes about our garden
Huffing and puffing
Moaning and groaning
Whistling and whining

Mum and I are inside
Our noses pressed against the glass
Watching, waiting
The giant shakes the trees
And sends the leaves flying through the air

At his feet
Small animals run to hide
Birds duck into their nests
And children
Pull covers over their terrified eyes
While the giant
Shakes their houses

But we aren't afraid
We are GIANT HUNTERS
Mum and I
And we won't stand for this
We pull on our armour
And take up our swords
Ready?
Mum looks at me
Waiting
Ready! I say
And out we go
Into the frenzy

Dan Next Door tries to keep us in
'You'll catch your deaths!'
He shouts
From the top window
But we don't listen
We roar
Our voices loud as a giant's
We roar and run
We rush and race
While the rain lashes
Pelting us with darts cold as ice

The giant tries to knock me over
But Mum grabs my hand
I wave my sword at him
Mum kicks up clouds of leaves
With her boots
The clothes dance on the clothes line

Crazy can-can dancers
Until the giant grabs them
And catapults them up into the scowling sky
Mum runs to rescue them

I see the giant capture our swing
And cast it into the air
I grab it
And climb on board
Up I go
Up on the giant's back
Flying through the air
Mum cheers
And opens her mouth
To drink the sweet cold rain
And we laugh
And laugh
And laugh

The giant is getting tired
Soon we can barely hear his angry roars
He stops blowing
A hurricane
And becomes a soft breeze
The rain he lashed at us
Is now a lazy plop
That sits on broad leaves
The giant tries one more time
But gutters, splutters and dies

All is quiet
A velvet silence
Falls on the garden
Nothing moves
And the birds begin to sing

Mum nods at me
Our work here is done!
She helps some sorry flowers to their feet
I splash in the water
That was freed from the pond
I hold Mum's hand
And we head back into the house

GIANT HUNTERS!
Safe again
Together

Ready for the next time
Ready for anything

The Gang

WRITTEN BY LISETTE AUTON
Illustrated by Elisa Paganelli

There's a bit at the bottom of the garden where the Gang hang out. Putnam wanted to call us the Spectral Investigators cos she likes ghosts. We argued and Aisling went home in tears because we all said, 'Hadaway!' to her Pink Sparkly Unicorns 'R' Us idea.

The next day, when they came back, and we all shook hands and spat over our left shoulders to make it better again, I said, 'The Gang's proper reet enuf, cos we're so good we divvent need anotha posh name.'

And that was it.

We drew the name out in pencil

first, just in case we forgot how to spell The Gang, and then painted it in yellow and orange. We'd used up all the other colours doing the underwater mural along the wall at the bottom. Aisling painted the dolphin on it. When she got to its eyes she kept saying, 'I'll just make 'em match,' an' they got bigga an' bigga . . . until Putnam took the paintbrush off her. We meant to paint over it when she wasn't looking, but we kind of liked that it was wonky.

I say garden. That's hedging the truth, as me nana would say. Not sure that's the propa phrase, like, but if Nana says it, it's right, or she'll stand behind the door and get the backs of your legs with the wooden spoon. That's another reason why using me wheelchair is mint; she cannot get at mine.

The garden is more of a concrete rectangle with occasional weedery which half passes for a flower. In fact, they are flowers. Don't know who gets to decide weeds are second-class plants. Not right that.

Can I tell you a secret? Promise you'll keep it for me?
Really promise?
If you wait long enough, the mural moves.
If you wait long enough, the mural invites you inside.

I haven't told the rest of the Gang yet, cos I wanna keep it all to meself for a bit. An' anyways, they're always saying to me, 'Oi, Davey Grout, stop tellin' tales!'

Then they listen, like. Cos I tell 'em good.

Spent a lot of years lying down flat, with just me nana lookin' after us, and I got good at making worlds in me head.

Then Putnam moved in next door and she waved at the window. And when I went out in me chair she just said, 'Nice wheels,' and that was it. Dead easy.

Don't know why I didn't think it'd be dead easy with her.

Be nice if everything was, if I didn't feel like a weed when I can't get into a shop or people talk to Nana instead of me. She's brill then, just says, 'You talk to him, ain't you got no manners?' Then she does this massive tut thing, and they go bright red and then talk to me. Free chocolate bars usually too. I share them with the Gang. Aisling calls it Pity Chocolate. Still tastes nice, mind.

It was last Thursday evening, the first time it happened. Nana was at bingo and it was nice out. Starlings along the fences and the sky bleeding red into the blue.

I'm sitting by the mural, bottle of pop, coupla custard creams, and blow me if the dolphin with the wonky eyes doesn't wink at me. At first I thought it was the streetlights coming on, but they were still dark.

Checked.

Looked back.

The dolphin's moved.

Taken its colour with it and left unpainted bricks behind, orange and cement.

It's right at the front, along the bottom, among the fish and the starfish that Putnam did in greens and blues. Right at my eye level.

And now I swear on me collection of dinosaurs that this next bit actually real-life happened.

'Fancy a swim?' the dolphin says.

'Me?' I say, lookin' around.

'Who else?' says the dolphin and shrugs. Didn't know a dolphin could shrug now, did ya?

An' I think to meself, *You know what, why not?*

But then I get shy, wonder if it hasn't noticed. Worry that when it does it'll just swim off. Me head is full of all the stuff people tell me I can't do. Full of all them steps and the weeds and the people who talk to Nana and not to me.

I point to me legs in the chair.

The dolphin shrugs.

And smiles.

My big dream is very strange – it's a wish machine. It's a brightly coloured machine shaped a bit like an arcade machine. It has a keyboard with flashing letters and a screen the size of a large iPad.

To use it, you simply type in your wish and it will show up on the screen. Before you press enter, you have to select a button for multiple wishes, otherwise it will shut down after one wish.

The wish machine has a 100% success rate, which means all the wishes come true. It will do exactly what you say, so you need to phrase it right. You also need to spell it right, otherwise the machine will not understand. It randomly travels around so it's extremely rare to see. Nobody has ever used it though as it's so hard to find – that's why nobody knows it exists.

ARTHUR, AGE 10,
ARDLEIGH ST MARY'S PRIMARY SCHOOL

THE GIANT Jumperee

WRITTEN BY JULIA DONALDSON
Illustrated by Helen Oxenbury

Rabbit was hopping to his burrow.

'Home sweet home,' said he.

Then he heard a voice, a loud, loud voice:

'Beware! Beware of me

Because . . .

I AM the Giant Jumperee.

I AM the Giant Jumperee.

I AM scary as can be.

I'm the Giant, Giant, Giant Jumperee.'

Cat slunk up to the burrow.

'I'll pounce on you,' said she.

Then she heard a voice, a loud, loud voice:

'Beware! Beware of me

Because . . .

I AM the Giant Jumperee.

I AM the Giant Jumperee.

I CAN squash you like a flea.

I'm the Giant, Giant, Giant Jumperee.'

Bear strode up to the burrow.

'I'll knock you down,' said he.

Then he heard a voice, a loud, loud voice:

'Beware! Beware of me

Because . . .

I AM the Giant Jumperee.

I AM the Giant Jumperee.

I CAN sting you like a bee.

I'm the Giant, Giant, Giant Jumperee.'

Elephant stomped to the burrow.

'I'll pick you up,' said he.

Then he heard a voice, a loud, loud voice:

'Beware! Beware of me

Because . . .

I AM the Giant Jumperee.

I AM the Giant Jumperee.

I AM taller than a tree.

I'm the Giant, Giant, Giant Jumperee.'

Frog jumped up to the burrow.

'I'm not scared,' said she.

Then she raised her voice, her croaky voice:

'Come out now, Jumperee,

Because . . .

YOU ARE the one we want to see.

YOU ARE the one we want to see.

WE ARE counting up to three,

Yes, we're counting, counting, counting up to three.

ONE, TWO, THREE!'

Cat, Bear, Elephant and Rabbit

Were scared as scared could be.

But then out there hopped a baby frog.

He was laughing, 'Tee-hee-hee!'

He said . . .

'HI, MUM, I'm the Giant Jumperee!

IT WAS only little me.

CAN WE all go back for tea

With the tiny little Giant Jumperee?'

Stanley's
SUPERSONIC VACUUM
WRITTEN BY GARETH PETER
Illustrated by Garry Parsons

Tidy Town was the tidiest place on earth. But Stanley was not a tidy boy. Everyone in Tidy Town liked things spick and span, neat and clean, ordered and arranged. But Stanley was an inventor. He was too busy designing cog-tastic devices to pick up after himself. He loved mess because it inspired him – after all, you never know where your next awesome idea will come from.

Tidy Town was not happy about Stanley's mess. So Mayor Sweep called a TOP-SECRET meeting.

'My classroom's in chaos!' barked Mrs Scrub the teacher.

'My library's like a bombsite!' moaned Mr Wipe the librarian. 'And it's all because of ONE boy.'

'Stanley!' they both roared.

'We must do everything we can!' said the Mayor. 'The town must stay tidy at ALL costs. Stanley will have to go to Cleaning Camp!'

But Stanley had been secretly listening. *I won't go. I'm going to invent my way out of this!* he thought to himself. That night he lay awake scribbling in his notebook, hoping an idea would catapult itself into his mind. But nothing did.

The next morning he was awoken by his dad.

'Stanley,' he called. 'Clean AND vacuum your room. You can't leave until it's done.'

'Blinking Bolts, I've got it!' cried Stanley. 'I'll make the most awesome vacuum . . . EVER. A super-sized, supersonic sucker! No Cleaning Camp for me.'

In secret, he assembled old toasters, frying pans, broken toenail clippers, even a cheese grater. And by the time the moon was up . . . it was ready.

He arranged his toys in a semicircle, put on a top hat and cleared his throat. 'I present the Supersonic Vacuum. Prepare to be dazzled as mess is eliminated at the flick of a switch . . .'

KER-WAZZZZ!

His vacuum guzzled up everything in his room. Toys, pants, even his notebook.

'Clanking Cogs!' shouted Stanley. 'It's too powerful, but at least there's no mess. Maybe I should try again.' So he heaved his machine outside, changed the setting and . . .

KER-MUNNNCH!

The machine gobbled up his dad's rose bush . . . then . . . next door's car, a lamp post, a passing cat and the entire contents of Mrs Scrub's garage.

'Wiggling Widgets!' he cried. 'It's still not quite right. I'll have one more go.'

So he hurried to the town square, made further adjustments and tried once again. The vacuum whirred and purred and gently gulped . . .

One tiny stone.

'Tidy-tastic,' said Stanley. But then . . .

KER-SLURRRP!

It sucked up the the town monument . . . then several trees, three cars, a fire engine, a boat from the harbour, the Pizza Parlour, the library books, and what appeared to be a large wall surrounding the town . . . a wall that had been hiding a secret.

'Stinking Socks!' shrieked Stanley, as a tidal wave of junk came flooding into the streets. Years of unwanted toys, apple cores, socks, toilet seats and every broken item imaginable had been hidden behind that wall. This was the real reason why Tidy Town had remained so impressively tidy.

'Our secret rubbish stash!' sobbed the Mayor, as a sparking lamp post crashed into the library, causing it to burst into flames.

'The town is in CHAOS,' cried Stanley. 'And it's my fault. I have to do something.' Then, like a comet, an idea flashed into his mind. He grabbed his machine and hurried to the swimming pool. Swiftly, it swigged up the water (and a few inflatables).

'With a few tweaks there . . .' said Stanley, zooming back. 'A waggle here, and . . .'

KER-SPLOSHHHH!

Stanley had reversed his machine and sent water gushing back out. The fire was extinguished and Tidy Town erupted in applause. And then . . .

. . . every library book came hurtling out . . . in alphabetical order. Out popped the Pizza Parlour, pizzas now assembled. Out exploded every car, boat, engine and tree back to their original positions . . . and out flew the town monument, gleaming and shinier than ever. **KER-FLOPPED!**

Stanley raced home and out everything else. And, purely by accident, he'd found the most perfect, tidy-tastic setting, as everything landed in a neat and ordered manner. For the first time his room was actually TIDY.

'Galloping Gadgets!' he said. 'I'll write that in my notebook.' But he couldn't find it.

Suddenly he had another brainwave. He bolted back to the town square and turned the machine to FULL POWER.

'Stand back,' he shouted.

The vacuum then crunched, munched and gobbled EVERY last piece of rubbish . . .

KER-CRUNCH-MUNCH-GOBBLE-SLURRRRP!

Tidy Town was once again astonishingly spotless.

'Amazing!' said Mayor Sweep. 'But . . . but what are we going to do with the rubbish?'

Stanley had thought of that . . . He twizzled the controls again, sending every piece rocketing back out – now scrubbed, sorted and squished into neat piles – ready to be reused.

'I'll be tidy . . .' he said. 'If Tidy Town finds useful and inventive ways to reuse its junk.' And with that, the machine coughed out his notebook.

KER-FLOOOP!

Stanley laughed. 'I guess keeping things tidy is important.'

Tidy Town continued to be spotless, but from then on, rather than hiding their junk, everyone did their best to recycle and reuse. Stanley didn't go to Cleaning Camp, and instead converted his bedroom into a workshop for inventing incredible new devices, starting with the world's most-delicious-cake-baking and most-smelly-stinky-sock-washing machines . . .

His workshop was tidy enough that things didn't get lost, but not TOO tidy – as a little bit of mess can inspire the most unexpected ideas!

Glowing
FOX TAILS

WRITTEN BY MARIA KUZNIAR
Illustrated by Katie Hickey

It was midnight somewhere over the Arctic and Claudia was the only one awake on the hushed plane. Her dad was snoring beside her and Claudia scowled at him – this was all his fault! If he hadn't got a new job in Norway, she wouldn't have had to say goodbye to her best friends and leave her chubby rabbit, Crumpet, behind.

'It's just for a year,' he had said, but that felt like forever. Yes, her grandparents would visit, but Crumpet couldn't fly on a plane and her friends would probably forget she existed. Her mum had said Claudia could stay with her and her stepfather, but Claudia loved the little family of two she and her father made, along with all their traditions – board-game night, stargazing and visiting the library every weekend. They even matched, with their chestnut hair and gingerbread-brown eyes.

She stared miserably out of the window. When they left London, soaring up, up, up, she'd imagined castles with turrets made out of cloud-stuff, marshmallowy moats and whipped-cream peaks. Now everything was dark and boring. She sighed and ate some chocolate buttons. Then the plane hit a patch of bumpy air and she heard a soft gasp behind her.

Claudia knelt up and peeked over the seat. A girl around her age was also awake, biting her nails, her eyes huge as moons.

'I'm s-scared of flying,' she whispered.

'Looking out of the window helps.' Claudia leaned over and pulled up her blind, hoping there'd be a twinkle of lights or something interesting.

There was a flash of bright green light.

Claudia's mouth fell open and she dropped her packet of buttons.

The other girl smiled and sat up. 'It's the aurora – the Northern Lights.'

The aurora ribboned through the night like shimmering emeralds.

'In Norway, our legends say that the lights come from the

armour of Vikings riding horses across the sky, but the Finnish myth is my favourite,' the girl said. 'They call the aurora the fire fox and believe that the foxes ran across the sky so fast that their tails glowed and sparked and lit up the night.'

'It's amazing,' Claudia said, staring out of the window. Her imagination fizzed to life. 'It looks like a sea of glittering fireflies!'

The other girl blinked. Claudia bit her lip, wondering if the girl would think she was weird – like all her new classmates probably would – but then she laughed and said, 'Or a wizard painting the night with magic!'

'Or fairies dancing through the sky in sparkling ice-gowns,' Claudia said, resting her arms on the seat back.

The other girl didn't seem to notice the odd jolt of the plane any more. 'Mermaids with seafoam scales swimming past the stars,' she said, her blue eyes gleaming.

'Ooh,' Claudia said, impressed. She thought hard for a moment. 'Frost elves building dazzling light-palaces!'

'Pixies sweeping stardust off the moon!'

'Cabin crew, take your seats for landing,' the pilot announced.

The Northern Lights melted away and disappeared. When they dipped lower, a city came into view. Pinpricks of light, and dark patches where Claudia knew the mountains and fjords slept. Snow tumbled past the windows.

'Tromsø,' the other girl said happily. 'This is my home.'

Claudia picked up her chocolate buttons and offered the packet. 'It's going to be my home this year, too. I'm Claudia,' she said a little shyly.

'Astrid,' the other girl said, taking some buttons. 'Will you be going to the international school?'

Claudia nodded, feeling nervous again.

Astrid beamed at her. 'That's where I go – everyone's really nice. Do you want to come over before school starts so I can tell you all about it? My mum makes the best hot chocolate, and we can go snowshoeing in the forest behind my house.'

Claudia smiled back. It sounded magical, like a winter wonderland. 'Yes please!' She began to think that maybe this year wouldn't be so bad after all.

THE GREAT
Imaginarium

WRITTEN BY RACHEL MORRISROE

Illustrated by Steven Lenton

Herr Brain's inventions were
daring and clever,
Made in his lab, with his
Labrador, Trevor.

A sweet multiplier, a fridge that cooked dinners,
A robot that taught ballroom dance for beginners.

And Trevor would help, with a pen in his jaws,
And special adapters for dexterous paws.

How Trevor would bark with such doggy delight,
To see, after years, an invention come right.

The dog and the world-famous octogenarian,
Were known, above all, for their IMAGINARIUM.

A wacky machine made of smelly old socks,
A tractor, some glitter, two grandfather clocks.

It tuned into airwaves of childhood ambition,
Powered by gerbils and nuclear fission.

It helped eager children to live out their glories.
A farmer, a doctor, a writer of stories.

But mean Dr Dobad was busily spying,
To get to the top of her game without trying.

She's greedy and grim as a poisonous weed,
'I'm Dobad by name, but I do worse in deed!'

She snuck to the lab, unscrewed
    bolts from the tractor,
Then spilled her hot chocolate inside
    the reactor.

She said (swapping gerbils for slugs from the yard),
'It's easy to cheat, only dummies try hard,

That dope and his doggy will soon be retiring!'
She hid round the back, once she'd messed up the wiring.

Next day, the machine started clunking and tapping,
As children made wishes, Herr Brain started flapping.

It shuddered and shook and flashed blindingly bright,
'Oh dear,' said a worried Herr Brain. *'Gesundheit!'*

They should have been happy; they should have
    been cheering,
But Herr Brain's invention had started mishearing . . .

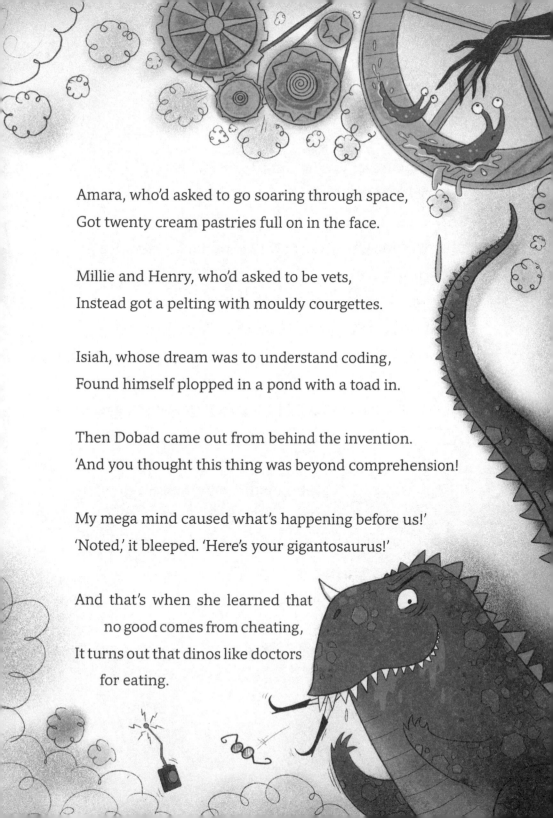

Amara, who'd asked to go soaring through space,
Got twenty cream pastries full on in the face.

Millie and Henry, who'd asked to be vets,
Instead got a pelting with mouldy courgettes.

Isiah, whose dream was to understand coding,
Found himself plopped in a pond with a toad in.

Then Dobad came out from behind the invention.
'And you thought this thing was beyond comprehension!

My mega mind caused what's happening before us!'
'Noted,' it bleeped. 'Here's your gigantosaurus!'

And that's when she learned that
        no good comes from cheating,
It turns out that dinos like doctors
        for eating.

Poor Trevor was howling, Herr Brain dried his tears,
'To fix this will take me another ten years!'

The hours whizzed by and his wrinkles grew deep.
He worked day and night and forgot about sleep.

Like white cotton candy his hair kept on growing.
He worked in the sunshine and when it was snowing.

Rewiring was hard, the hot chocolate had stained,
And Trevor found slugs are not keen to be trained.

Until, on the radio, one afternoon,
Herr Brain heard Amara had flown to
the moon!

He danced with delight and the dog gave a
yelp.
'She did it!' he shouted. 'And without
our help!

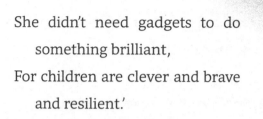

She didn't need gadgets to do
    something brilliant,
For children are clever and brave
    and resilient.'

He grinned as the astronaut
    spoke to the nation,
'Herr Brain and his dog are my
    true inspiration!'

And though their invention was no longer needed,
As Trevor gave paw, an idea was seeded.

'It's taken some failures to know, in the end,
My dream is to understand you, my old friend!'

He rewired the tractor and plugged in a speaker,
Then to his amazement, his dog barked, 'Eureka!'

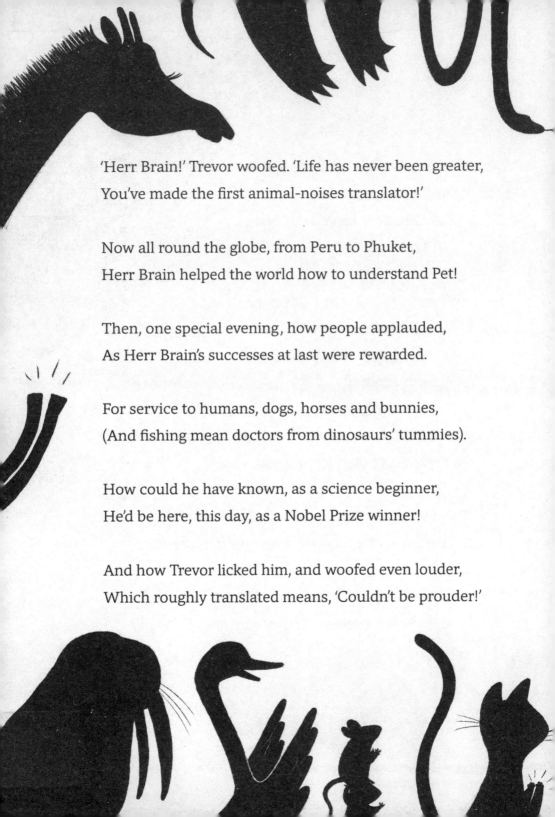

'Herr Brain!' Trevor woofed. 'Life has never been greater,
You've made the first animal-noises translator!'

Now all round the globe, from Peru to Phuket,
Herr Brain helped the world how to understand Pet!

Then, one special evening, how people applauded,
As Herr Brain's successes at last were rewarded.

For service to humans, dogs, horses and bunnies,
(And fishing mean doctors from dinosaurs' tummies).

How could he have known, as a science beginner,
He'd be here, this day, as a Nobel Prize winner!

And how Trevor licked him, and woofed even louder,
Which roughly translated means, 'Couldn't be prouder!'

THE *Ocean* OF STORY

WRITTEN BY NAZNEEN AHMED

Illustrated by Areeba Siddique

Sumaya had explored every inch of the library and every single one of the books on the shelves.

Or so she had thought.

One morning, Sumaya's mum headed to the computers, as she did every time, to write her job applications. They visited every Saturday without fail, and every day during the school holidays. Sumaya knew it was because it was too expensive to heat their flat through the day, and there wasn't anywhere else to go that didn't cost money.

Sumaya sighed. Her world was so small: just the flat, her school, the library. She decided to go down to Geography, perhaps because she wanted to be somewhere, anywhere, else. Running her fingers across the white and steel railings, she made her way down the steps.

She lugged a dusty old atlas on to the turquoise carpet and traced the places Ma had told her their family came from. Peshawar . . . Lahore . . . Chittagong. The names sounded full of mystery and promise, but Sumaya had never even been to the Isle of Wight.

Then something on one of the lower shelves caught her eye.

A tiny book, covered in aquamarine leather, tucked between two old books.

She pulled it out and opened it. It was strange: it didn't have words or maps on the pages, just curious shapes with  dates inside them. The clocktower bells began to ring out, marking ten. Sumaya started to turn the pages in time, reaching page ten on the final ring.

At that very moment, a strange breeze whipped through the library, and everything around her began to move.

First, the book-shelves and the wooden door flew through the air and

stacked themselves neatly underneath Sumaya's feet. Then the railings rose up, shaped themselves into an arch and lowered themselves on to the doorframe. The long white curtains and curtain pole spun away from the window and planted themselves into the wood of the door. It all happened very smoothly, like a dance.

'It's been a long time since my last voyage,' rumbled a deep, rolling voice from the timbers.

Sumaya jumped. Where walls had been a few moments ago, there was sky. She looked down, and realized she was now standing on the deck of a ship that seemed to be talking to her. She ran to the railing and looked overboard. Where the carpet had just been, there was now a turquoise sea.

Panic flooded her stomach.

'What do you mean, voyage? Where are you taking me? Where's my mother?' she cried.

'The library will return at noon. You opened the book at page ten on the tenth toll. That doesn't happen very often, you know.'

She still had the book in her hand. She flicked through the pages and looked again at the shapes. They were stamps. The last, over twenty years ago, was in the shape of a pirate's hat.

'That child wanted to visit Treasure Island. I can go to any river, lake or ocean that's in any of the books in the library. Sumaya, where would you like to go?'

She sucked her breath in hard. There were so many places. Breathing out, she whispered, 'Peshawar.'

'And which Peshawar would you like to visit?'

Sumaya frowned. 'There's more than one?'

'Each book's places are unique to it. Do you wish to go to the Peshawar in a geology book, in military history, or in the 1901 atlas you were just looking at?'

'The atlas, please.'

The ship moved smoothly across the water, slicing through the waves. In a few moments the turquoise darkened to a muddy olive colour, and riverbanks rose on either side. Dark grey-green mountains reared sharply above.

'The Great Kabul River,' announced the ship.

A plank lowered itself to the bank. Sumaya clambered down, her whole body humming with excitement. She started climbing the rocks until she could see the tops of the mountains. She spied little huts balanced improbably among the peaks. *Our family must live somewhere nearby*, Sumaya thought, her arms tingling. She had imagined an exotic place scented with rosewater and cardamom, but the real Peshawar was fierce and wild. To live here, her relatives must be fierce and wild too. Despite the crisp breeze, pride glowed warm in her chest.

'Sumaya, it is time to return,' came the ship's voice.

It had felt like no time at all, two hours. She felt a rush of sadness as they sped away.

'Where to next time, Sumaya?' the ship rumbled gently, as she watched the waters turn turquoise again.

'Next time?'

But the ship didn't answer. Sumaya looked up to find the library back to normal.

She sighed. It wasn't the first time she'd fallen asleep in the library.

But she still had the book in her hands. She flicked through the pages. On the last page there was a new stamp: this year's date, inside the shape of a tiny mountain.

She looked at the bookshelves and smiled. Now she could go anywhere she wanted, even the Isle of Wight. All she needed was the right book.

The Dog who
DANCED ON THE MOON

WRITTEN BY JOHN BOYNE
Illustrated by David Roberts

There once was a boy called Jeremy Lump,
His mum was a nightmare, his dad was a grump.
He didn't have too many friends of his own
Except for his dog, who would twerk for a bone.

The dog was called Maxwell and danced like a dream.
He hoped to do *Strictly* but couldn't get seen
By producers who only liked showbusiness folk
And thought twerking dogs would be seen as a joke.

At school, teachers laughed right in Jeremy's face
When he said that his dream was to venture through space
And meet different species and alien tribes.
Poor Jeremy had to ignore all their jibes.

'When I'm a grown man, in my twenties or more,'
said Jeremy, raising his eyes from the floor,
'I can be what I want, an inventor or cook.
I can write a great screenplay, a song or a book,

I can climb every mountain, design better tyres,
I can sail 'cross the oceans, or fight forest fires.
I can be what I want, I could even cure cancer,
And Maxwell could yet be a *Strictly Come* dancer.'

The dog did a twerk, then the robot, the jive.
He danced 'cross the room and he gave a high five
To Jeremy, who was a very good master.
He got so excited he danced even faster.

And later, at home, though they both felt quite tired

They nevertheless felt completely inspired

To follow their dreams, get a job, volunteer,

As a great dancing dog and a space pioneer.

Fast-forward in time, let's say ten, fifteen years,

When Jeremy still dreams of final frontiers

And Maxwell, despite all the time that's advancing,

Is somehow still breathing and somehow still dancing.

An ad in the paper says 'Astronauts Wanted,

Some brave men and women, not easily daunted,

Who'll give up five years for a long travelogue,

And yes, if you like, bring your cat or your dog.'

It didn't take long for the pair to apply,

They got through the interviews, tests, said goodbye

To their friends and their loved ones and soon

      were installed

On a spaceship the rocket designers had called

Apollo 500. It soared through the sky
At remarkable rates, flying ever so high,
Its occupants wondering what they might find
When they reached unknown parts, leaving
      Earth far behind.

The people who'd once said the boy was a fool,
His parents, his teachers, the pupils at school,
All had to think twice when they followed his pattern
Of travels, from Earth to Mars, Neptune and Saturn.

And as for brave Maxwell, his brilliant CV
May not have delivered a spot on TV
But the animal kingdom all fell in a swoon
When they read of the first dog who
      danced on the moon.

Dream Smaller

WRITTEN BY NATALIA O'HARA

Illustrated by Lauren O'Hara

On the morning of his eighth birthday, little Izzy Blick had a dream. Nobody in the Blick family had ever seen one before, so Izzy did not know what it was – this bright and hairy thing that crawled out of his ear, sneezed, and danced in the crack of his library book.

When Izzy came downstairs his mother said, 'No dreams at the dinner table, Isaiah.' And his father said, 'Just don't feed it. If you feed them they keep coming back.'

After that, Izzy's parents tried not to see the rapidly growing multicoloured hairball in their house. And when

they did see the dream, they tidied it.
Into the toybox, or the bin, or – on one
unlucky day – the washing basket.

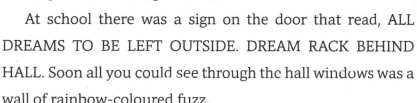

And it grew so fast. 'If that whale gets
any bigger . . .' muttered Izzy's father.

So Izzy started making a Not-to-Do
List of the things that made his dream
grow. Comic books, the sea, hugs, new
shoes, paints, kittens, grandma, dinosaurs . . .

At school there was a sign on the door that read, ALL
DREAMS TO BE LEFT OUTSIDE. DREAM RACK BEHIND
HALL. Soon all you could see through the hall windows was a
wall of rainbow-coloured fuzz.

'The crazy thing is running wild,' Izzy's father said one
night after his son had gone to bed. 'This morning I saw it
laying eggs in the compost.'

'A child that small with a dream so big! It's not safe,'
his mother complained. 'Who knows where that thing could
drag him?'

When I was 7¾, my big dream was to be a firefighter, rushing into burning buildings, saving people from disaster areas, rescuing cats from trees, being an all-round hero . . . but then, with a fear of heights, I had to rethink!

Then I found myself reading Roald Dahl and my mind went in all directions: anything can happen, be it imaginary or real. My life could be whatever I wanted it to be and whatever I wanted to make of it. *Charlie and the Chocolate Factory* inspired me with a passion for chocolate — eating lots of it at that young age! I dreamed of building my own chocolate factory with everything edible, picking chocolate off trees just like in the book. This developed into baking and cookery into a career that has served me well and hopefully helped to inspire others . . .

ASHLEY McCARTHY, EXTREME CHOCOLATIER

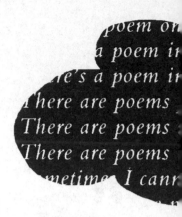

Poetics

FROM

TALKING TURKEYS

WRITTEN BY BENJAMIN ZEPHANIAH
Illustrated by The Point

There's a poem on your face
There's a poem in the sky
There's a poem in outta space
There are poems passing by,
There are poems in your dreams
There are poems in your head
Sometimes I cannot get to sleep
Cause there are poems in me bed.

There are poems in me tea
There are poems on me toast
I have found much poetry
In the place I love the most,

There's a poem right in front of you
Get to know its rhyme,
If you are not sure what to do
Just call it poem time.

There's a poem in me shoes
There's a poem in me shirt
When the poem meets the blues
It can really, really hurt,
Other poems make you grin
When they dribble off your chin
Some poems think they are great
So they like to make you . . .

Wait
I see poems in your teeth
I see poems in me cat
I hear poems underneath
Going rata tat tat tat,
This one has not finished yet
It keeps coming on the beat
It is soggy and it's wet
But it's also very sweet.

There are poems for the ear
There are poems for the page
Some poems are not quite clear
But they get better with age,
There are poems for the hip
There are poems for the hop
Everything is poetic
Poetry will never stop.

There are poems on your fingers
There's a poem on your nose
If you give it time to linger
It will grow and grow and grow,
There's a poem in you beautiful
Can't you see it
It's right

There,
I think it's so incredible
There are poems
Everywhere.

My big dream is nearly impossible. It's out of this world, literally. It's mind-blowing! It's a flying donkey powered by its own gas. It would fly to the moon with a flag with a donkey on it that says 'first donkey to land on the moon'. We would be all over the news and I would be so excited. We would fly all over the world and even pay the ISS (International Space Station) a visit and meet another flying donkey (that is nowhere near as cool as us) who buys us a pair of cool-dude glasses and then joins us on our travels.

As well as flying, my donkey will find he has a new talent: if he burps, he flies in reverse. It would be awesome if we couldn't feel any part of our bodies because if we crashed we wouldn't feel any pain. After our flying expedition had lasted 48 years, we would go home to England and be greeted by a crowd of 100,000 people who would be waiting to interview us. It would go amazingly!

So, when you are lying in bed and wondering what we're doing, just look out of your window and give us a wave.

LUCY, AGE 11,
ARDLEIGH ST MARY'S PRIMARY SCHOOL

My big dream is to become an archaeologist. I want to gather fossils to collect DNA to bring dinosaurs back to life. I want to do this so we can learn how they lived. We can find out if they were dangerous to humans. I would use a big forest full of grass and trees for them to live in. I would work with scientists to mix dinosaurs' DNA with other animals' like monkeys to clone new animals. I would try using the DNA from the Gallimimus because they are small and fast.

If I mixed this with a monkey's, my creature could run fast and we could hold it. I would call it monkeysaurus.

RYAN, AGE 7,
ST GABRIEL'S CATHOLIC PRIMARY SCHOOL

DREAM *Bold*

THE A-Z OF *Amazing*

WRITTEN BY RASHMI SIRDESHPANDE
Illustrated by Diane Ewen

A is for **AMAZING**. It's what you are. Don't let anyone tell you otherwise.

B is for **BEING**. Being present, right here, right this moment.

C is for **CURIOSITY** and forever learning.

D is for **DREAMING** and dreaming BIG.

E is for **ELEVATING** your mind and your thoughts.

F is for **FUN**. There's a lot of that to be had in this incredible world.

G is for **GRATITUDE**. However hard life may seem, there are a thousand things to be grateful for.

H is for **HAPPINESS**, and finding it in the littlest things.

I is for **INSPIRATION**. It's *everywhere*.

J is for **JUSTICE** and standing by what is fair and right.

K is for **KINDNESS**. One small sprinkle can change everything.

L is for **LOVE** and how it moves the whole world.

M is for **MOVEMENT**, and making time for it every single day.

N is for **NEVER EVER EVER EVER** giving up.

O is for **OPPORTUNITY**. Finding it but also *creating* it!

P is for **PERSISTENCE** and making things happen.

Q is for **QUIET** and how calmness brings out creativity.

R is for **RESILIENCE**. You'll need it when times are tough. And there may well be times like that.

S is for **SMILING**. Do this. Lots. It's contagious.

T is for **TRUST** . . . in yourself, in the universe. Even if it doesn't always seem that way to you, it's got your back.

U is for **UNITY**, and knowing we're stronger together.

V is for **VISION**. Imagining the difference you can make to your life and the lives of others.

W is for **WONDER**, the most magical feeling. Something so beautiful you can't put it into words.

X . . . Well, **X MARKS THE SPOT**. There's great treasure to be found in this world – you just have to look.

Y is for **YOU** and being **YOURSELF**. Because no one does it better.

Z is for **ZEST** and **ZING** and bringing that brilliant energy to everything you do in this one wonderful life. It's all we've got. Let's make it a good one.

The Three Fossils

FROM

BALLET SHOES

WRITTEN BY NOEL STREATFEILD

Illustrated by Ruth Gervis

'I do envy you. I should think it an adventure to have a name like that, and sisters by accident. The three of you might make the name of Fossil really important, really worth while, and if you do, it's all your own. Now, if I make Jakes really worth while, people will say I take after my grandfather or something.'

Pauline sipped her drink. It was very hot, but simply heavenly – the sort of drink certain to make a cold feel better. She looked across at Doctor Jakes over the rim of the glass, her eyes shining.

'Do you suppose me and Petrova and Posy could make Fossil an important sort of name?'

'Of course. Making your name worth while is a very nice thing to do; it means you must have given distinguished service to your country in some way.'

Pauline gave another gulp at her drink. She frowned thoughtfully.

'I don't think we do the things that make names important. I sew, and Petrova's awfully good at works of things – she can mend clocks and she knows heaps about aeroplanes and motor-cars. Posy doesn't do much yet.'

'There's time. You probably won't develop a talent till you are fourteen or fifteen. Are you good at lessons?'

'Well, we were. Petrova was very good at sums, and I said poetry the best in the class; but it's different now we learn with Garnie. You know, she has to teach Posy too, and she has to do the baby things, like learning her letters and it takes a lot of time. Petrova does sums well still, but Garnie just puts R.R.R; she never teaches her a new one. I say poetry sometimes, but not very often now.'

'What sort of poetry do you like?'

'All sorts. We learnt "Oh, to be in England" and "The Ancient Mariner", and I had just started "Hiawatha".'

'Do you ever learn any Shakespeare?'

'No. I should have started "As You Like It" the next term if

I had stayed at Cromwell House.'

'You should learn him. He wrote a few good parts for children. If you are fond of reciting, that's the stuff to work at.' She went over to her shelves and picked out a book, and opened it. 'Listen.'

She read the scene in 'King John' between Prince Arthur and Hubert. Pauline did not understand it all, but Doctor Jakes was one of those people who really can read out loud. Pauline forgot to drink her ginger, and instead, listened so hard that at last Doctor Jakes vanished, and in her place she saw a cowering little boy pleading for his eyes.

'There.' Doctor Jakes closed the book. 'Learn that. Learn to play Prince Arthur so that we cringe at the hot irons just as he does, and then you can talk about reciting.' She got another book, found the place and passed it to Pauline. 'You read me that.'

It was Puck's speech which begins 'Fairy, thou speak'st aright.' Pauline had never seen it before, and she halted over some of the words, but she got a remarkable amount of the feeling of Puck into it. When she had finished, Doctor Jakes nodded at her in a pleased way.

'Good! We'll read some more one day. I'll make a Shakespearean of you.'

Pauline heard the front door slam and got up. 'There's the others, I must go. Thank you very much for the ginger drink.'

'Goodbye.' Doctor Jakes did not look up; she was studying 'A Midsummer Night's Dream'. 'Don't forget, it's fun having a name with no background. Tell the other Fossils.'

After tea Pauline told Petrova and Posy what Doctor Jakes had said. Petrova was most impressed.

'Do you think she meant we could make it a name in history books?'

Pauline was not sure.

'She didn't exactly say history books, but I think that's what she meant. She said making your name worth while means you must have given distinguished service to your country.'

Petrova's eyes shone.

'How lovely if we could! Fancy people learning about us as lessons! Let's make a vow to make Fossil a name like that.'

Pauline looked serious.

'A real vow, do you mean, like at christenings?'

'Yes.' Petrova hopped, she was so excited. 'Like "promise and vow three things . . ."'

'What about her?' Pauline pointed at Posy, who, not understanding the conversation, was dressing her Teddy bear.

'Posy' – Petrova knelt down beside her – 'do you know what making a vow is?'

'No.' Posy held out a little pair of blue trousers. 'These don't fit Teddy any more.'

Pauline took Teddy and his clothes from her.

'You must listen, Posy,' she said in a very grown-up voice. 'This is important. A vow is a promise; it's a thing when you've made it you've got to do it. Do you understand?'

'Yes.' Posy held out her hand. 'Give me Teddy.'

'No.' Petrova took her hand. 'Not till we've finished the vowing.' She turned to Pauline. 'You say it, and Posy and I will hold up our hands and say "We vow".'

Pauline put both her feet together and folded her hands.

'We three Fossils,' she said in a church voice, 'vow to try and put our names in history books because it's our very own and nobody can say it's because of our grandfathers.'

She made a face at Petrova, who hurriedly held up her right arm, and grabbed Posy's and held it up too.

'We vow.' She said this so low down in her inside that it sounded terribly impressive, then she whispered to Posy, 'Go on, say "We vow".'

'We vow.'

Posy tried to say it in the same deep voice as Petrova, but she did it wrong, and it sounded rather like a cat meowing. This made them all laugh, and the big vowing, instead of ending seriously, found them laughing so much that they fell on the floor, and their tummies ached.

Pauline was the first to recover.

'Oh, we oughtn't to have laughed!' She wiped her eyes. 'But, Posy, you did sound silly!' She gave another gurgle. 'Shall we make this same vow over again on each of our birthdays?'

'Let's,' agreed Petrova. 'It'll make our birthdays so important.'

'We vow,' Posy said in exactly the same meow. This time they could not stop laughing, and they were still giggling when it was time to go down to be read to by Sylvia.

Kandaka

WRITTEN BY YASSMIN ABDEL–MAGIED

Illustrated by Soufeina Hamed

Asmaa adjusted the straps of her backpack on her shoulders and sighed. The blue school bag was full of textbooks and sports gear, weighing heavily on her back as she walked to the bus stop.

It had been a long day for Asmaa, a lanky dark-skinned hijabi girl who had just started at a new school. Her family had moved from London to the countryside, but this new village was nothing like Tottenham. For a start, there was nowhere for Asmaa and her three sisters to get their hair done! Also, people wouldn't stop staring at them, no matter where they went. To make matters worse, she had failed to make the basketball team. Tryouts that afternoon had been miserable: she was the last to be picked for a team, then no one would pass to her; then, when she eventually did get a chance to shoot, she missed. It was like the countryside had sucked the life out of her: Asmaa was the best basketball player on her whole block back home, but somehow she had lost her spark.

That evening, Asmaa's parents and siblings tried to cheer her up, but had no luck. Without basketball, who was she? She went straight to her room after dinner and curled up on her bed.

'Asmaa, *habiba*,' her mum said softly, as she gently pushed the door open and sat next to her daughter on the bed. 'I'm sorry the basketball didn't work out. *Khair*, maybe you can try another sport?'

Asmaa kissed her teeth and shuffled round, facing the wall away from her mother.

'*Mafi mushkilla*,' her mum said, using the Sudanese phrase for 'no worries'. 'Anyway, I've brought you a special jalabeeya to wear to bed tonight. My mama gave it to me when we left Sudan. It's got a bit of magic in it . . .'

Asmaa's mum left the jalabeeya, the simple Sudanese outfit that looked like a loose, brightly coloured nightgown, on the bed, then walked out. After a few minutes Asmaa wiped the tears off her face and changed into the outfit.

Oh, it was so smooth! The golden material shimmered slightly as Asmaa slid it on over her head, and a strange calm enveloped her, like a warm hug. She suddenly felt sleepy, quickly getting under the covers and closing her eyes.

Almost immediately, Asmaa began to dream. She saw a woman in front of her: a tall, regal lady who looked like a queen with a large, golden turban on her head. The queen stretched out her hands and beckoned towards Asmaa.

'What's going on?' she asked the figure, but the woman simply raised a finger to her lips, telling Asmaa to be quiet, and then motioned for her to follow. Asmaa's ghost self stepped forward, and then, almost immediately, everything went white.

Asmaa opened her eyes and realized she wasn't in her bed any more, but lying on the floor in a strange building made out of stone. She got up hurriedly, and went outside. The bright light blinded her for a moment, before she saw that she was inside one of the pictures on the wall in their house: she was in Merowe, Sudan . . . in the year 500 BC. She had just *time travelled! Whoa . . .*

Sky-high pyramids and pillars stood around her, with soft Sahara sand swirling in the air. From where she stood,

Asmaa could see that the city stretched for miles . . . *I can't believe this!*

The queen appeared beside her again. 'Asmaa,' she said, her voice deep and powerful. 'Look around you. This is where you are from. You have the power of thousands of years of strong Nubian women in your veins. Do not let anybody make you feel small. Never forget who you are. Never forget where you are from.'

Asmaa nodded, taking it all in.

'*Never forget who you are . . .*

'*Never forget where you are from . . .*'

'*Never forget, never forget,*' Asmaa murmured under her breath.

'Asmaa? Asmaa? Who are you talking to, Asmaa?'

Asmaa opened her eyes again, to the sound of all three of her younger sisters shaking her awake. She looked down. The jalabeeya had turned a dark brown colour; it no longer had the golden shimmer of the night before. Asmaa frowned, remembering her dream. Was it a dream? What had just happened?

Then, like a whisper carried on the wind, Asmaa heard the voice again. 'Never forget . . .' filled the room, and she knew that something special really had happened. Asmaa smiled to herself. Oh, she was going to get on to that basketball team all right. And athletics. And debating. She might even join the rowing team. There was no stopping her now. Her spark had returned.

This village had a queen in its midst. They. Weren't. Ready.

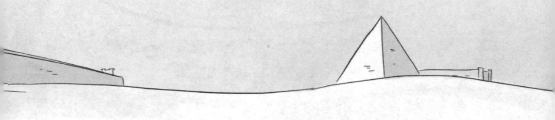

Lobot

FROM

WONDER

Written and illustrated by
R. J. PALACIO

Ever since I was little, the doctors told my parents that someday I'd need hearing aids. I don't know why this always freaked me out a bit: maybe because anything to do with my ears bothers me a lot.

My hearing was getting worse, but I hadn't told anyone about it. The ocean sound that was always in my head had been getting louder. It was drowning out people's voices, like I was underwater. I couldn't hear teachers if I sat in the back of the class. But I knew if I told Mom or Dad about it, I'd end up with hearing aids—and I was hoping I could make it through the fifth grade without having that happen.

But then in my annual checkup in October I flunked the audiology test and the doctor was like, 'Dude, it's time.' And he sent me to a special ear doctor who took impressions of my ears.

Out of all my features, my ears are the ones I hate the most. They're like tiny closed fists on the sides of my face. They're too low on my head, too. They look like squashed pieces of pizza dough sticking out of the top of my neck or something. Okay, maybe I'm exaggerating a little. But I really hate them.

When the ear doctor first pulled the hearing aids out for me and Mom to look at, I groaned.

'I am not wearing that thing,' I announced, folding my arms in front of me.

'I know they probably look kind of big,' said the ear doctor, 'but we had to attach them to the headband because we had no other way of making them so they'd stay in your ears.'

See, normal hearing aids usually have a part that wraps around the outer ear to hold the inner bud in place. But in my case, since I don't have outer ears, they had to put the earbuds on this heavy-duty headband that was supposed to wrap around the back of my head.

'I can't wear that, Mom,' I whined.

'You'll hardly notice them,' said Mom, trying to be cheerful. 'They look like headphones.'

'Headphones? Look at them, Mom!' I said angrily. 'I'll look like Lobot!'

'Which one is Lobot?' said Mom calmly.

'Lobot?' The ear doctor smiled as he looked at the headphones and made some adjustments. '*The Empire Strikes Back*? The bald guy with the cool bionic radio-transmitter thing that wraps around the back of his skull?'

'I'm drawing a blank,' said Mom.

'You know *Star Wars* stuff?' I asked the ear doctor.

'Know *Star Wars* stuff?' he answered, slipping the thing over my head. 'I practically invented *Star Wars* stuff!' He leaned back in his chair to see how the headband fit and then took it off again.

'Now, Auggie, I want to explain what all this is,' he said, pointing to the different parts of one of the hearing aids. 'This curved piece of plastic over here connects to the tubing on the ear mold. That's why we took those impressions back in December, so that this part that goes inside your ear fits nice and snug. This part here is called the tone hook, okay? And this thing is the special part we've attached to this cradle here.'

'The Lobot part,' I said miserably.

'Hey, Lobot is cool,' said the ear doctor. 'It's not like we're saying you're going to look like Jar Jar, you know? That would be bad.' He slid the earphones on my head again carefully. 'There you go, August. So how's that?'

'Totally uncomfortable!' I said.

'You'll get used to them very quickly,' he said.

I looked in the mirror. My eyes started tearing up. All I saw were these tubes jutting out from either side of my head—like antennas.

'Do I really have to wear this, Mom?' I said, trying not to cry. 'I hate them. They don't make any difference!'

'Give it a second, buddy,' said the doctor. 'I haven't even turned them on yet. Wait until you hear the difference: you'll want to wear them.'

'No I won't!'

And then he turned them on.

HEARING BRIGHTLY

How can I describe what I heard when the doctor turned on my hearing aids? Or what I didn't hear? It's too hard to think of words. The ocean just wasn't living inside my head anymore. It was gone. I could hear sounds like shiny lights in my brain.

It was like when you're in a room where one of the lightbulbs on the ceiling isn't working, but you don't realize how dark it is until someone changes the lightbulb and then you're like, whoa, it's so bright in here! I don't know if there's a word that means the same as 'bright' in terms of hearing, but I wish I knew one, because my ears were hearing brightly now.

'How does it sound, Auggie?' said the ear doctor. 'Can you hear me okay, buddy?'

I looked at him and smiled but I didn't answer.

'Sweetie, do you hear anything different?' said Mom.

'You don't have to shout, Mom.' I nodded happily.

'Are you hearing better?' asked the ear doctor.

'I don't hear that noise anymore,' I answered. 'It's so quiet in my ears.'

'The white noise is gone,' he said, nodding. He looked at me and winked. 'I told you you'd like what you heard, August.' He made more adjustments on the left hearing aid.

'Does it sound very different, love?' Mom asked.

'Yeah.' I nodded. 'It sounds . . . lighter.'

'That's because you have bionic hearing now, buddy,' said the ear doctor, adjusting the right side. 'Now touch here.' He put my hand behind the hearing aid. 'Do you feel that? That's the volume. You have to find the volume that works for you.

We're going to do that next. Well, what do you think?' He picked up a small mirror and had me look in the big mirror at how the hearing aids looked in the back. My hair covered most of the headband. The only part that peeked out was the tubing.

'Are you okay with your new bionic Lobot hearing aids?' the ear doctor asked, looking in the mirror at me.

'Yeah,' I said. 'Thank you.'

'Thank you so much, Dr. James,' said Mom.

The first day I showed up at school with the hearing aids, I thought kids would make a big deal about it. But no one did. Summer was glad I could hear better, and Jack said it made me look like an FBI agent or something. But that was it. Mr. Browne asked me about it in English class, but it wasn't like, what the heck is that thing on your head?! It was more like, 'If you ever need me to repeat something, Auggie, make sure you tell me, okay?'

Now that I look back, I don't know why I was so stressed about it all this time. Funny how sometimes you worry a lot about something and it turns out to be nothing.

When I was 7 ¾, I dreamed of a world in which there were no rules. I never liked rules. I just didn't understand them. Why couldn't I eat pudding before dinner? Why did I have to go to bed at 7? Why couldn't I grow wings and fly? Why? Why? Why?

I saw a world in which people used rules as an excuse to stop being curious; to stop asking 'Why?' They prevented people from thinking differently and creatively. The rules stopped people dreaming big!

I didn't know then that I was going to break lots of rules. People said that someone as little as me couldn't be a firefighter – because I didn't fit in that box. But I am one now! They told me that firefighters couldn't be scientists. But I'm one of those too. I tried to think about things differently, and it made me feel free. So next time someone reminds you that there are rules, don't forget that you're allowed to ask them: Why?

SABRINA COHEN-HATTON, FIREFIGHTER

Do A Project

FROM

PLEASE MRS BUTLER

WRITTEN BY ALLAN AHLBERG

Illustrated by Fritz Wegner

Do a project on dinosaurs.

Do a project on sport.

Do a project on the Empire State Building,

The Eiffel Tower,

The Blackpool Tower,

The top of a bus.

Ride a project on horses.

Suck a project on sweets.

Play a project on the piano.

Chop a project on trees

Down.

Write a project on paper,
A plaster cast,
The back of an envelope,
The head of a pin.

Write a project on the Great Wall of China,
Hadrian's Wall,
The playground wall,
Mrs Wall.

Do a project in pencil,
In ink,
In half an hour,
In bed,
Instead
of something else,
In verse,
Or worse;
Do a project in playtime.

Do a project on your hands and knees,
Your head,
With one arm tied behind you.

Do a project wearing handcuffs,

In a steel coffin,

Eighty feet down

At the bottom of the Hudson River

(Which ideally should be frozen over),

On Houdini.

Forget a project on Memory;

And refuse one on Obedience.

My big dream is to become an extraordinary footballer because it is all I ever wanted to do in my life. If I become a footballer I will play for Real Madrid. If I win the Ballon d'Or I will be so delighted because it is a rare achievement.

I will play with Ryan, Alex and Joshua.

Winning the World Cup, playing for Real Madrid, playing for Newcastle – which should I do?

Football is an immersive game: I love playing it.

The more I try, the more I have a chance.

This is my dream.

TONY, AGE 10,
ST OSWALD'S CE VA PRIMARY SCHOOL

The Good Boy

Written and illustrated by
ED VERE

Listen up, kid, it's good you're here. But get one thing straight: this ain't no walk in the park – it's a tough gig. It's not for everyone. Long days, longer nights.

You want to relax in front of a fire in the evening? Forget about it. It ain't that type a gig. You gotta be relentless . . . you gotta be chasing down the leads. Capiche?

I'll break it down for ya, nice and easy . . . A lotta mutts get a lot a big ideas about this job. A lot think they're cut out for it – not so many are. We get all sorts giving it a shot. Thoroughbreds to mongrels. You name it . . . Danes, labradoodles, chihuahuas. We had a Border collie come by just the other day.

It don't matter who you are, kid. We all bring something different to this game. We all got different talents. Just don't try acting the big shot . . . it won't suit ya, kid. You're young, there's a lot to learn.

It's like this, kid. You get a scent, you follow it. Never give it up. Like a dog with a bone. But make no mistake, kid – these ain't no bones we're talking about. This is serious business. Deadly serious . . . Understand?

There'll be a lotta leads takin' you in a lotta directions. Can you find the right one? Not everyone's got those kinda smarts.

Maybe you'll get a nose for it. Maybe you won't. Don't take it hard if you don't make the grade, kid . . . not many do.

I'll tell ya straight, kid – it's a crazy, messed-up world out there. And clients? They're as different as the stars in heaven. But they all got one thing in common: they lose their stuff . . . then they want that stuff back again. That's why we're here. We track stuff down. We do it quick. We deliver.

So you think you got the chops for this line of work, young pup? We'll see. You got a shot, like everyone else. Now go get some shut-eye . . . you'll need it.

Meet me here at dawn. We'll take a walk. Don't be late.

OK, kid, this is your big chance . . .

FETCH!

Good boy! Who's a good, good boy? You are . . . Yes, you are!

You did good, kid – you used your nose . . . you tracked it down and handled it like a pro. I ain't seen speed like that in years. Who knows, soon you could be chasing these things down every day. That means happy clients, kid. A lotta clients getting those sticks back . . . And maybe one day we'll understand why they keep losing them.

Until that day, welcome to the bureau, friend. Give yourself a pat. Not everyone gets to call themselves Private Investigator at the Federal Bureau of Lost Sticks and Missing Tennis Balls.

A Transformation

FROM

GOODNIGHT MISTER TOM

WRITTEN BY MICHELLE MAGORIAN

Illustrated by Alexis Deacon

One winter afternoon, while they were rehearsing, something happened which stunned everyone involved in the play.

Willie had already helped paint the scenery but had been asked to take over as prompter when Matthew Browne had been suddenly whisked off to boarding school.

He usually sat with the prompt book, next to Miss Thorne. His head still spun slightly as he followed the words and looked upwards intermittently to see by the expression of a face if someone had forgotten their lines. But after a while he soon knew large chunks of the play off by heart and could occasionally prompt without looking at the book. It was

difficult at first. Initially he whispered the line, but it was embarrassing to have to continually repeat himself after a series of 'pardons?' and 'whats?' and he soon discovered that if he spoke a line clearly and loudly he wasn't noticed as much.

On this particular afternoon Willie sat as usual with the prompt book resting on his knees, his forehead frowned into a tense concentration. The blackouts were already pulled down over the hall windows. Willie liked it that way. It gave an air of mystery and excitement to the rehearsals.

Carrie was the only one on stage. She stood with her hands

clasped tightly together and stared frantically at the curtain rail, her face racked with pain.

'Carrie, dear,' said Miss Thorne, 'you look as though you've got wind.'

'It ent fair,' she retorted, scowling fiercely.

'Isn't,' corrected Miss Thorne.

'It isn't fair,' said Carrie. 'I feels daft pretendin' to speak to someone who ent, isn't, there.'

Miss Thorne gave a sigh. Her long willowy legs splayed outwards into a balletic second. Although she was terribly fond of the children she found that working with them was like banging her head against a brick wall. Zach was the only one who showed any real talent and he was more of a performer than an actor. He played himself all the time, using his characters to display his many theatrical talents. He was still trying to persuade her to have a tap routine in the play.

She stared up at Carrie, slapping her forehead with the palm of her hand.

'Has anyone seen Christine or Robert King?' she asked, turning to the others who were sitting at the back of the hall.

'No, miss,' piped Lucy.

Robert was playing Scrooge.

'We'll do the crone scene then.'

'Christine's in that,' chorused three at the back.

'So she is,' said Miss Thorne. 'This really is too bad. We've two weeks to go and we are nowhere near being ready.'

She glanced at Willie.

'William, stand in for Christine.'

'But it's a girl's part,' said George.

'Well, we'll just have to have a male crone for today,' replied

Miss Thorne in a dangerously quiet voice.

Willie crept nervously on stage with the prompt book in his hand and was joined by the others.

'Begin!'

He read out Christine's part, giving an imitation of all the inflections in her voice, at the same time prompting those around him when they forgot their lines.

'No, no, no!' cried Miss Thorne. She looked around. 'Someone else prompt.'

'But then he won't be able to say his lines,' said Carrie.

'Er, will he?' she added nervously as Miss Thorne glared threateningly at her.

'I'll prompt,' said Zach.

Miss Thorne didn't think this was too good an idea but time was precious, so she agreed.

'Now, William,' she said. 'Do you think you can remember the moves?'

He shrugged helplessly.

'Well, let's try, shall we? And William?'

'Yes, miss?'

'Imagine that it's very cold and dark, that you're old and hungry and that you love stealing and making trouble for people.'

Willie looked at her dreamily.

'Did you hear that?'

He nodded.

'Good. You have the first line. Start when you're ready.'

'Ready?' he asked, feeling a little puzzled.

'When you feel that you're that horrible old man.'

Willie withdrew into himself. He remembered an old tramp he used to watch down by the Tube station near where he lived. He was hunched and he dragged his feet when he walked. He also remembered times when he himself was so hungry that he couldn't stand straight for the cramps in his stomach.

Miss Thorne watched him grow visibly older. His shoulders were pushed up by his neck and his stomach caved in. He looked cold and miserable and bad-tempered.

Zach found himself totally mesmerized and placed his finger on the page so that he wouldn't lose his place.

Then Willie began speaking. His voice was harsh and mean. The others on stage stared at him and someone giggled.

'Carry on,' interrupted Miss Thorne firmly.

The three on stage with Willie joined in as best they could, but they sounded as if they were reading out lines from

a school book. Willie carried on imagining that his dirty feet were wrapped in rags and newspapers and when the scene came to an end he shuffled slowly off the stage.

'I say,' whispered Zach.

'You'll say nothing for the moment,' said Miss Thorne.

'Let's do that scene again. You're beginning to get the idea, William.'

They rehearsed the scene over and over again and as they repeated it Willie believed more than ever that he was the old man. He found himself suddenly reaching out and touching someone or making some wild arm movement without thinking. He didn't understand what Miss Thorne meant when she told him to keep a gesture. How could he keep something that just happened?

When Miss Thorne finished working on the scene he heard his companions sigh with relief.

'I'm fair done in,' one of them said.

How strange, he thought, I'm not tired at all. I could easily have gone on.

He came down the tiny steps at the side of the stage and sat beside Zach.

'You're good,' whispered Zach.

'Good? How d'you mean?'

'You're a good actor.'

Willie didn't understand. He thought that being an actor was tap dancing and playing the fool. All he'd done was to make a picture of someone in his head and worm his way inside it.

He took the prompt book back from Zach and began his old job again.

For the next half hour the rehearsals took on a sudden lift and everyone began to dare to try things out without feeling foolish. The only thing that spoilt it was the absence of Robert. He was in nearly all the scenes. Finally Miss Thorne refused to wait any longer and told them to take a short break while she left the hall to make a phone call to Hillbrook Farm.

Willie found himself immediately surrounded. Lucy slipped her hand into his. He flushed and pulled it away.

'Dunno what you're on about,' he said quietly in response to their praise. 'I jest pretended I was someone else, that's all.'

'I really believed you was that horrible old man,' said Carrie in admiration.

But so did I, thought Willie. He was puzzled. He didn't understand why they were making so much fuss.

'You're a natural,' said Zach. 'When you talked it was like

you'd just thought of it. How did you do it?'

'I jest listened to what someone said and answered them, like.'

All the sudden admiration unnerved him. He felt lonely being so different. To hide his fear he asked Zach to tell a joke and do his funny buffalo step. Zach hesitated at first, but luckily someone who hadn't seen him do any tap dancing egged him on. Willie was soon forgotten, and became mixed into the group again.

Zach stopped. He heard Miss Thorne open the outer door of the hall. She flung the inside door to one side, was about to slam it but changed her mind and closed it behind her in a quiet and controlled manner. Her face was pale and she was wringing her hands in agitation.

'Sit down everyone, please.'

They did so immediately.

She walked slowly towards her chair, sat down, folded one leg over the other and placed her clasped hands over her knee.

'I'm afraid I've just had some rather bad news. Robert and Christine's mother came early this morning and took them back to London. It seems she felt they were being used as unpaid labour. This means that we have no Scrooge.'

'Oh no!' cried Zach amidst the loud wails of disappointment.

'Does that mean we can't do it?' asked Carrie. There were only two weeks till the performance. They had all helped with scenery and costumes. Did this mean that all their hard work was wasted?

Miss Thorne turned to Willie.

'William,' she said quietly. 'I'd like you to play the part of Scrooge.'

Willie felt an intense tingle pass from his toes to the roots of his hair. He looked up at her. Everyone's face was turned to him as if he was their last chance.

'Will you?'

He nodded.

'Oh, well done,' cried Zach. 'Hip, hip, hurray!'

'That's enough,' interrupted Miss Thorne firmly. 'We have a lot of work to do. We'll start with Act One, Scene One. Those not in the scene will have to take turns prompting. We must all pull together and help.'

She turned to face Willie. He was standing quite still, feeling both paralysed and yet at the same time filled with a flood of energy.

'Don't hurry,' she said.

'Everythin' has its own time,' he whispered and he blushed. 'That's what Mister Tom ses.'

I open my eyes and find myself sitting in front of a huge desk. The sun is shining directly on my face and I notice the room I am in. All the furniture is wooden but the walls are empty, not a single picture is up. Suddenly, the door flings open and a lot of people rush into the room, all speaking to me at once.

As Mayor, I have to sign many papers all day and everybody asks me to do lots of things! For example, getting rid of guns, knives, crimes; my dream is to make sure there are no more gangs fighting and killing each other. I especially want children to be safe. I'm always very busy and never get that much sleep at night. I was so tired. Suddenly I heard a loud noise.

I woke up and my alarm was ringing for school. It was all a dream, but I will make sure when I grow up that I will be Mayor. I will study a lot in school to make London a better place for everyone!

NAZIFA, CHRISTCHURCH PRIMARY SCHOOL

A Terrific Pig

FROM

CHARLOTTE'S WEB

WRITTEN BY E. B. WHITE

Illustrated by Garth Williams

Far into the night, while the other creatures slept, Charlotte worked on her web. First she ripped out a few of the orb lines near the centre. She left the radial lines alone, as they were needed for support. As she worked, her eight legs were a great help to her. So were her teeth. She loved to weave and she was an expert at it. When she had finished ripping things out, her web looked something like this:

A spider can produce several kinds of thread. She uses a dry, tough thread for foundation lines, and she uses a sticky thread for snare lines – the ones that catch and hold insects. Charlotte decided to use her dry thread for writing the new message.

'If I write the word TERRIFIC with sticky thread,' she thought, 'every bug that comes along will get stuck in it and spoil the effect.'

'Now let's see, the first letter is T.' Charlotte climbed to a point at the top of the left-hand side of the web. Swinging her spinnerets into position, she attached her thread and then dropped down. As she dropped, her spinning tubes went into action and she let out thread. At the bottom, she attached the thread. This formed the upright part of the letter T. Charlotte was not satisfied, however. She climbed up and made another attachment, right next to the first. Then she carried the line down, so that she had a double line instead of a single line. 'It will show up better if I make the whole thing with double lines.'

She climbed back up, moved over about an inch to the left, touched her spinnerets to the web, and then carried a line across to the right, forming the top of the T. She repeated this, making it double. Her eight legs were very busy helping.

'Now for the E!'

Charlotte got so interested in her work, she began to talk to herself, as though to cheer herself on. If you had been sitting quietly in the barn cellar that evening, you would have heard something like this:

'Now for the R! Up we go! Attach! Descend! Pay out line! Whoa! Attach! Good! Up you go! Repeat! Attach! Descend! Pay out line. Whoa, girl! Steady now! Attach! Climb! Attach! Over to the right! Pay out line! Attach! Now right and down and swing that loop and around and around! Now in to the left! Attach! Climb! Repeat! OK! Easy, keep those lines together! Now, then, out and down for the leg of the R! Pay out line! Whoa! Attach! Ascend! Repeat! Good girl!'

And so, talking to herself, the spider worked at her difficult task. When it was completed, she felt hungry. She ate a small bug that she had been saving. Then she slept.

Next morning, Wilbur arose and stood beneath the web. He breathed the morning air into his lungs. Drops of dew, catching the sun, made the web stand out clearly. When Lurvy arrived with breakfast, there was the handsome pig, and over him, woven neatly in block letters, was the word TERRIFIC. Another miracle.

Lurvy rushed and called Mr Zuckerman. Mr Zuckerman

rushed and called Mrs Zuckerman. Mrs Zuckerman ran to the phone and called the Arables. The Arables climbed into their truck and hurried over. Everybody stood at the pigpen and stared at the web and read the word, over and over, while Wilbur, who really felt terrific, stood quietly swelling out his

chest and swinging his snout from side to side.

'Terrific!' breathed Zuckerman, in joyful admiration. 'Edith, you better phone the reporter on the *Weekly Chronicle* and tell him what has happened. He will want to know about this. He may want to bring a photographer. There isn't a pig in the whole state that is as terrific as our pig.'

The news spread. People who had journeyed to see Wilbur when he was 'some pig' came back again to see him now that he was 'terrific'.

My big dream is to be a professional motor-cross rider. The bike of my dreams is a KTM 250cc. Currently I ride a 110cc pit bike which doesn't go as fast as the KTM. My dream bike would have a customized race-tuned engine (this is when mechanics make the exhaust sound louder and better). My dream KTM would be orange and blue.

The track that I am going to ride has a main track and a beginners' track with fewer bumps. I would like to ride it every day, but would really only be able to ride it once or twice a week as I would have a full-time job as a mechanic so that I could do my own repairs. I would race at the weekends, and when I get spotted I would be picked up by a sponsor and get my bike upgraded and new gear – jersey, trousers, boots and helmet all in my team colours.
This would be my dream come true.

OSCAR, AGE 11, THE RAMSEY ACADEMY

MY BROTHER GETS
Letters

WRITTEN BY MICHAEL ROSEN

Illustrated by Anna Doherty

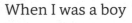

When I was a boy
I noticed that my brother used to get letters.
I didn't get any.
None at all.
When his friends went on holiday,
they sent him postcards and jokes and
he'd sit there, laughing and pointing at them.
'Yeah . . . hee hee . . . really good.'

Sometimes he'd get a letter
from someone he didn't even know:
the letter said it was an 'offer' –
something going cheap or even for free.

But me,
I got nothing.
Nothing at all.
And I was jealous of him.

Until one day I was looking at the newspaper
and there was an ad for some special
Memory Course.
They would help you find what they called your
'Inner Mind Force'.
And down the bottom,
down at the very bottom,
    there was a little form.

        You had to fill in your name and address,
      send it off,
            and you'd get a letter back telling you how
              you would find your Inner Mind Force.

        Simple as that.
      Fill in the form with my name and address.
      Sit and wait.
        And I'd get a letter!

Now of course
I wasn't that bothered about my
Inner Mind Force.
What I wanted was a letter.
And that's exactly what they promised.
I'd get a letter.

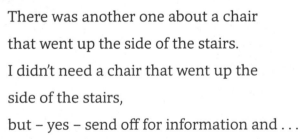

Then I looked for some more.
There was one on how to cure baldness.
I was only nine years old and I wasn't bald,
but send off for information –
and I'd get a letter.

There was another one about a chair
that went up the side of the stairs.
I didn't need a chair that went up the
side of the stairs,
but – yes – send off for information and . . .
I'd get a letter.

And there were some more
and I sent them all off.
Secretly.
I didn't tell anyone.

Then I went up to my brother
and said really casually:
'Hey, I bet – out of us two
I get more letters than you.'
He said, 'What?!
What are you talking about?
No one writes to you.
You never get any letters.'
'OK,' I said, 'let's see.
We'll keep a score.
Me and you. See who gets more.'

'Great,' he said, shaking my hand. 'Done!'
'Oh, hang on,' I said. 'What do I get when I've won?'

'No prizes,' he says,
'but whoever loses has to do whatever the winner
says.'

He must have thought I was crazy
to have taken him on.
He was dead sure he would win.

Inside I was so excited.
I thought: *I can't wait to see his face*
when these letters start turning up.

Well, I didn't have to wait long.

The first to arrive was a letter
with an ad to do with bodybuilding.

'There you are,' I said to my brother.
'A letter! That's one–nil.'

He sat there reading the ad.
'Rippling muscles – on guarantee –
measure your progress on our unique
power meter!'

I waited for my next letter.

Next day, it arrived.

It was one about dieting.
There was a whole load of stuff
about some Miracle Pills.
I didn't read the rest:
'Two–nil! I'm winning, aren't I?' I said to my brother.
He was starting to get really annoyed
with me and my letters.

Next day, there were two more.
Two more!
There was a very glossy booklet
on a Pension Plan

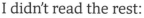

and another one on Shoes for the Larger Man.

For three days, my brother hadn't got anything
in the post.
We sat opposite each other at the breakfast table.

'Four–nil now!' I said.

'D'you want to give in?

You see? They're coming in every day now.'

And sure enough – not long after

something did arrive.

But it wasn't quite what I was expecting.

It was a great big parcel.

It had come from Liverpool.

'Who's it for?' I said.

'Look! Here!' said my dad, pointing at the address:

'You!'

I couldn't believe it:

It was the first parcel I'd ever had.

'Go on, open it,' he said.

It was wrapped in red paper.

I peeled it off.

There was a big brown cardboard box.

I pulled the lid off, and inside

was the thing we used to have on our beds

before duvets were invented.

They look pretty much the same.

It was called an 'eiderdown'.

An eiderdown!

'Who sent it?' my dad said.

'I don't know,' I said.

'How much did it cost you?'

'It didn't cost me anything.

They just sent it.'

I was panicking.

Remember, I was only nine years old.

'Did you send off for this thing, or not?'
my dad said.

'No,' I said, 'I just filled in some form.

It said there was something for free.

Fill in the form and it'd just come.'

'*Meshuggene!*' he says (it means 'crazy' in Yiddish).
'They mean the eiderdown
is free for seven days.
If you don't want it, you have to send it back.
Keep it longer than that, you have to pay.
But what were you doing?' my father said.
'I wanted a letter,' I said.
I felt such an idiot looking at the eiderdown.
I looked at my brother. He looked back.
'What's the matter?' he said. 'Five–nil! Well done.'
He laughed.

'So you'll wrap up the box and send it back?'
Dad says.
'Unless you want to pay
for a new eiderdown for your bed.'

But – you know,
I didn't do it straight away,
I didn't do it the next day,

or the next. Or the next.
The eiderdown and the wrapping were sitting
in the corner of the room in a gigantic mess.

I'm thinking: *The eiderdown's growing.*
No, hang on, the box is shrinking . . .

Anyway, four days went by,
and I still hadn't sent the eiderdown back.
We were all having our tea
and the doorbell went.

Dad went to see who was there.
We could hear voices coming from the door.
Moments later, he was back,
looking very serious, straight at me.
'It's for you,' he says.

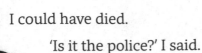

I could have died.

'Is it the police?' I said.

'Do they want to know about the eiderdown?'

'No,' he said. 'There's a man out there.

He's got something for you.'

'What do you mean?

Men don't come round with stuff for ME.'

But I went to the door,
and they all followed behind me to see
what it was all about.

There was a man there with a black notebook
in his hand.
He looked down at it.
'M. Rosen, is it?' he said.
I said, 'Yes, M. Rosen, that's me.'
So he says, 'Right, then.
It's outside – shall I wheel it in?'
'What?' I said.
'The washing machine.'
'Washing machine?!!!' I said. 'Oh no, that's not for me.'
'Well, it says here, "M. Rosen". Do you want to see?'

'No,' I said. 'I only send off for free things.'

'Yes,' he said. 'The demonstrations are for free,

but not the washing machines.'

'I don't want it,' I said.

I looked round for help from the others.

You can imagine how I felt.

But they were hiding behind the door.

Laughing their heads off as quietly as they could.

I turned back. Looked up at the man.

'It's in the van,' he said.

'I've brought it all the way from Harlesden

to show it to you,' he said.

'No!' I said.

'No?' he said. 'Isn't there anyone else

I could show it to?'

He looked down at me.

I looked down at my feet.

Then he just shut his book and went,

and I shut the door behind him.

And straight away my brother was in there with:

'Shall I add that to your score?

Six–nil. Have you won yet?'

I said, 'I think I've had enough of this letters bet.'

And he said, 'Why? What's the matter?

Don't you want a washing machine?

You could use it to keep your eiderdown clean!'

Oh no! The eiderdown!

For a moment I'd forgotten about it.

'I can't pack it into the box,' I said. 'It's . . . it's . . .'

But Mum said, 'Don't worry, I'll help you send it back,

though what's coming next? A bed?'

Dad said, 'Hang on, what's happened here?
This bet . . . who's won the bet?
And what does the winner get?'

My brother looked really happy and said,
'I've lost. No, I've got to hand it to him.
He gets the most. And that means he gets to choose
what I have to do for him.'
'All I want,' I said, 'is, I don't want to hear any more
about it.
If I have to send off to get a letter,
I'm better off without it.'
'OK, OK, OK,' my brother said. 'Let's call it square.
'Great,' I said. 'Let's call it square.'

But even now,
when there's someone who calls round
for me at the door
and my brother answers it,
he'll call out,
'Hey, Mick, it's for you.
Someone here has got
an eiderdown for you!'

THE Joys OF WRITING

FROM

CHINESE CINDERELLA

WRITTEN BY ADELINE YEN MAH

Illustrated by Eileen Kai Hing Kwan

I grew even closer to my aunt. Our room became my refuge. Coming home from school every afternoon, I was ever so glad to cross its threshold, close the door, and spread out my books. Doing homework was the only way to cushion me from the harrowing uncertainties all around.

I knew Niang loathed me and despised my aunt. It saddened me that Aunt Baba seemed to be under a life sentence of subordination. Though I was little, I understood the awkwardness of her position: how Niang's wishes always took precedence, how she had to demonstrate caution, submission and humility at every turn.

I found it impossible to speak of this. It was simply too painful.

Instead, I tried to make it up to my aunt by studying hard and getting perfect report cards. Besides, that seemed to be the only way to please my father or get any attention from him whatsoever.

I was seven years old and in the second grade. The girls in my class nicknamed me 'Genius' – partly because of my perfect scholastic record, but also because of my compositions and short stories.

I started writing by accident. Mrs Lin, my teacher in Chinese literature whose daughter Lin Tao-tao was my classmate, once gave our class a homework assignment: to write a composition titled 'My Best Friend'. Most girls wrote about their mothers. I didn't know mine so I wrote of my aunt.

My aunt and I share a room. She is my best friend and cares about me in every way. Not only about my hair, my clothes and how I look; but also about my studies, my thoughts and who I am. Though I am really nothing, she makes me believe I am special. When I get a good report card, she locks it in her safe-deposit box, and wears the key around her neck even when she sleeps, as if my grades were her most cherished treasures.

My mama and my aunt used to be best friends. Sometimes I dream of my mama on my walks to and from school. I think

Mama lives high up on a mountain in a magic castle. One day, if I am really good and study very hard, she will ride down on a cloud to rescue me and take me to live with her. Nothing in Shanghai can compare with her place. It's a fairyland full of fragrant flowers, towering pines, lovely rocks, soaring bamboos and chirping birds. Every child can enter without a ticket and girls are treated the same as boys. No one is sneered at or scolded without a reason. It's called Paradise.

Mrs Lin gave me a high mark and pinned my composition on the bulletin board. From then on, I wrote whenever I had a spare moment. It thrilled me to bring my literary efforts to school, and to see my classmates pass them illicitly from desk to desk. Groups of girls would gather around me during recess to discuss my stories, or to hear me read aloud the latest escapades of my imaginary heroines.

To me, writing was pure pleasure. It thrilled me to be able to escape the horrors of my daily life in such a simple way. When I wrote, I forgot that I was the unwanted daughter who had caused my mother's death. I could be anybody I wished to be. In my narratives, I poured out everything that I dared not say out loud in real life. I was friends with the beautiful princesses and dashing knights who lived in my imagination.

I was no longer the lonely little girl bullied by her siblings. Instead I was the female warrior Mulan who would rescue her aunt and Ye Ye from harm.

Good Pig

FROM

THE SHEEP-PIG

WRITTEN BY DICK KING-SMITH
Illustrated by Ann Kronheimer

'I want to be a sheep-pig,' he said.

'Ha ha!' bleated a big lamb standing next to Ma. 'Ha ha ha-a-a-a-a!'

'Bide quiet!' said Ma sharply, swinging her head to give the lamb a thumping butt in the side. 'That ain't nothing to laugh at.' Raising her voice, she addressed the flock.

'Listen to me, all you ewes,' she said, 'and lambs too. This young chap was kind to me, like I told you, when I were poorly. And I told him, if he was to ask me to go somewhere or do something, politely, like he would, why, I'd be only too delighted. We ain't stupid, I told him, all we do want is to be treated right, and we'm as bright as the next beast, we are.'

'We are!' chorused the flock. 'We are! We are! We a-a-a-a-a-are!'

'Right then,' said Ma. 'What shall us do, Babe?' Babe looked across towards Farmer Hogget, who had opened the gate of the collecting-pen and now stood leaning on his crook, Fly at his feet. The pen was in the left bottom corner of the paddock, and so Babe expected, and at that moment got, the command 'Come by, Pig!' to send him left and so behind the sheep and thus turn them down towards the corner.

He cleared his throat. 'If I might ask a great favour of you,' he said hurriedly, 'could you all please be kind enough to walk down to that gate where the farmer is standing, and to go through it? Take your time, please, there's absolutely no rush.'

A look of pure contentment passed over the faces of the flock, and with one accord they turned and walked across the paddock, Babe a few paces in their rear. Sedately they walked, and steadily, over to the corner, through the gate, into the pen, and then stood quietly waiting. No one broke ranks or tried to slip away, no one pushed or shoved, there was no noise or fuss. From the oldest to the youngest, they went in like lambs.

Then at last a gentle murmur broke out as everyone in different ways quietly expressed their pleasure.

'Babe!' said Fly to the pig. 'That was quite beautifully done, dear!'

'Thank you so much!' said Babe to the sheep. 'You did that so nicely!'

'Ta!' said the sheep. 'Ta! Ta! Ta-a-a-a-a-a! 'Tis a pleasure to work for such a little gennulman!' And Ma added, 'You'll make a wunnerful sheep-pig, young un, or my name's not Ma-a-a-a-a-a.'

As for Farmer Hogget, he heard none of this, so wrapped up was he in his own thoughts. He's as good as a dog, he told himself excitedly, he's better than a dog, than any dog! I wonder . . . !

'Good Pig,' he said.

Then he uncrossed his fingers and closed the gate.

A Powerful Gift

FROM

THE DARK IS RISING

WRITTEN BY SUSAN COOPER

Illustrated by Joe McLaren

'My name is Merriman Lyon,' he said. 'I greet you, Will Stanton. We have been waiting for you for a long time.'

'I know you,' Will said. 'I mean . . . you look . . . I felt . . . don't I know you?'

'In a sense,' Merriman said. 'You and I are, shall we say, similar. We were born with the same gift, and for the same high purpose. And you are in this place at this moment, Will, to begin to understand what that purpose is. But first you must be taught about the gift.'

Everything seemed to be running too far, too fast. 'I don't understand,' Will said, looking at the strong, intent face in alarm. 'I haven't any gift, really I haven't. I mean there's nothing special about me.' He looked from one to the other of them, figures alternately lit and shadowed by the dancing flames of candles and fire, and he began to feel a rising fear, a sense of being trapped. He said, 'It's just the things that have been happening to me, that's all.'

'Think back, and remember some of those things,' the old lady said. 'Today is your birthday. Midwinter Day, your eleventh Midwinter's Day. Think back to yesterday, your tenth Midwinter's Eve, before you first saw the sign. Was there nothing special at all, then? Nothing new?'

Will thought. 'The animals were scared of me,' he said reluctantly. 'And the birds perhaps. But it didn't seem to mean anything at the time.'

'And if you had a radio or a television set switched on in the house,' Merriman said, 'it behaved oddly whenever you went near it.'

Will stared at him. 'The radio did keep making noises. How did you know that? I thought it was sunspots or something.'

Merriman smiled. 'In a way. In a way.' Then he was sombre again. 'Listen now. The gift I speak of, it is a power, that I will show you. It is the power of the Old Ones, who are as old as this land and older even than that. You were born to inherit it, Will, when you came to the end of your tenth year. On the night before your birthday, it was beginning to wake, and now on the day of your birth it is free, flowering, fully grown. But it is still confused and unchannelled because you are not in proper control of it yet. You must be trained to handle it, before it can fall into its true pattern and accomplish the quest for which you are here. Don't look so prickly, boy. Stand up. I'll show you what it can do.'

KEEP FLYING, Little Bird!

WRITTEN BY BEN LERWILL

Illustrated by Chris Wormell

With a swoop and a lift and a glide and a drift, Little Bird came in to land.

She had a black head, short legs and long, graceful wings. She was just ten weeks old, but when she flew, SHE FLEW.

Little Bird was an Arctic tern. She had hatched on an island called Greenland near the North Pole, but she would soon be spreading her wings. For the first time, she would be flying to her other home.

Her other home was Antarctica, at the very bottom of the world.

Every year, Little Bird's mother and father flew from the top of the world to the bottom. And every year they flew back again. Like Little Bird, her parents were small, but their silver-tipped wings were strong.

The journey would be hard for such a young bird. It would be long, tiring and dangerous.

But it was time. The three birds turned away from the mountains and faced the ocean. And, with a swoop and a lift and a glide and a drift, their journey began.

Her mother and father swept upwards. Little Bird followed, light as a seashell. They climbed into the silent sky, and they flew.

They flew south, soaring above the waves. Sometimes Little Bird rose so high that all she could hear was the wind. And sometimes she flew so low that she could catch fish to eat.

Sunrise followed sunrise. All was ocean, as far as the eye could see.

But after a time they found no fish to eat. For two days, then three, they went hungry. Little Bird flew more slowly. She grew so tired that she could barely lift her wings.

On the fourth day, a shoal of silver fish appeared, a gleam in the blue. Her father arrowed into the waves.

He came out with a herring in his beak. Her mother plunged into the sea, and Little Bird followed. They found fish, and they fed. Now Little Bird flew on, much stronger.

The days blew by. One cloudless afternoon, a month after leaving Greenland, Little Bird dipped her wings and sped low. When she flew back up high, she saw something new. Something big. Land in the distance.

It was Africa.

Little Bird reached the shoreline. She flew in loops and dived for fish. For days the three birds travelled south past purple volcanoes and dazzling bays. They crossed the equator on hot winds. Every day was long, and rich with light.

One morning, just as Little Bird had gathered a fish from the waves, a sea eagle flashed out of the sky. It rushed at her, snatching with its talons.

Little Bird turned swiftly in the air, but her fish fell. The eagle caught it, gobbling it down in one gulp.

The three tiny birds flew on, fluttering in panic then finding quiet. Every day they glided through the endless blue, staying close to land. Until one morning when, as quickly as Africa had appeared in front of them, it disappeared behind them.

Then it was ocean, and more ocean. The birds were weary. But still they flew.

The waves swelled and the winds rushed. The seas were darker now, and the air wilder. Little Bird soared on. Her great journey was nearly over.

And on a blustery, sunny afternoon at the bottom of the world, it happened. The three birds saw their southern home shining white in the distance. They sailed through the sky, with 10,000 miles trailing out behind them. Shelves of ice filled the horizon.

The sun shone. They tilted their wings towards the shoreline. For the first time, Little Bird felt the great white breath of Antarctica. And, with a swoop and a lift and a glide and a drift, she came in to land.

Her journey was over. In a few months, when the freezing cold set in, she would take to the air again. But for now, under the golden polar sun, Little Bird rested.

My dream is to play for the English rugby team. I love sports and sleeping. So I would be very happy to play for England. After that, I would appreciate a nap. I also play cricket and I like cricket, but not as much as rugby.

I know that if I want my dream to come true, I will have to work hard during training on all my rugby skills, making sure I am fast and strong. I need to make sure I eat all the right things to fuel all my hard work in training. I need to eat proteins and vitamins and food full of energy.

I would like to play for the Newcastle Falcons one day. I think this will help me achieve my dreams as they have lots of talented players that I can learn from. I will hopefully play for England Under 18s and then carry on through to play for the England first team. I hope to play for England in the World Cup in 2027. If we win, I will be the youngest winner ever.

That is my dream . . .

LUCAS, AGE 7, INGS FARM PRIMARY SCHOOL

written and illustrated by
KRISTINA STEPHENSON

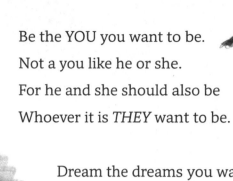

Be the YOU you want to be.
Not a you like he or she.
For he and she should also be
Whoever it is *THEY* want to be.

Dream the dreams you want to dream,
No matter how different those dreams may seem.
For that's what dreams are meant to be,
Different for you and he and she.

Don't let anyone say: 'You can't!'
'You're silly!'
'You'll never!'
'You're daft!'
'You shan't!'

If you have a dream, then you *can* be . . .
Whatever sort of YOU
you want to be.

High Hopes

FROM

FIRST PRIZE FOR THE WORST WITCH

written and illustrated by
JILL MURPHY

On the last day of Summer Term there was a ceremony called Fourth Year Firsts, when prizes were awarded to pupils who had proved themselves best in certain subjects over the past four years. It was also the occasion when the witch chosen to be Head Girl for the coming year would be solemnly announced. This event was actually more important to the girls than the final year itself, when there would be no time for distractions, as everyone would be working madly to pass the Witches' Higher Certificate.

'Have you got any hopes for Fourth Year Firsts?' asked Maud, passing Mildred a chocolate biscuit as they coasted along smoothly, cloaks and hair streaming behind them in the wind.

'Not *exactly*,' replied Mildred. 'What about you? Tell me yours and then I'll tell you mine.'

'Well,' said Maud, 'I'm sort of average at everything, but there *is* a First Prize for Team Spirit, so I'm going to work on that one – you know, being extra helpful and so on. What about you?'

'If I tell you what I'd like to get,' confided Mildred, smiling shyly at her friend, 'you have to promise not to laugh.'

'Cross my heart!' promised Maud.

'OK then,' said Mildred. 'It isn't *exactly* a first prize, more of an honour, but it would be the only first prize that I would want.'

'Go on!' urged Maud, intrigued. 'Tell me!'

'You mustn't laugh!' Mildred reminded her.

'My word is my bond,' said Maud, looking at Mildred with a very serious face.

'Right,' announced Mildred. 'I'd like to be chosen as Head Girl for next year.'

Maud really did try to keep her serious face on, but almost immediately she erupted into such peals of laughter that she nearly fell off her broom.

'You promised not to laugh!' exclaimed Mildred indignantly. However, within seconds she was drawn into Maud's infectious and unstoppable fit of giggles, and soon the two of them were doubled over on their broomsticks, desperately trying to steer and keep their balance.

'It isn't *that* funny!' snorted Mildred. 'I have done quite a few good things for the school, in between disasters!'

Maud was now laughing so much that tears streamed down her cheeks and blew away in the wind. 'Sorry, Mil!' she howled. 'It's just so incredibly un*likely*.'

I was always writing stories and drawing pictures, and trying them out on my toys as you can see from this picture — they were very attentive!

JILL MURPHY

When I was 7¾ I had two big dreams for the future: to write books about all of the characters and stories in my head and to own a pet snake. Now I am 31¾, I spend my life writing books and I own a pet lizard – I think I've done pretty well!

ROBIN STEVENS, AUTHOR, AGE 31¾

JOURNEY TO
Dream Country

FROM

THE BFG

WRITTEN BY ROALD DAHL

Illustrated by Quentin Blake

Every minute, the mist became thicker. The air became colder still and everything became paler and paler until soon there was nothing but grey and white all around them. They were in a country of swirling mists and ghostly vapours. There was some sort of grass underfoot but it was not green. It was ashy grey. There was no sign of a living creature and no sound at all except for the soft thud of the BFG's footsteps as he hurtled on through the fog.

Suddenly he stopped. 'We is here at last!' he announced. He bent down and lifted Sophie from his pocket and put her on the ground. She was still in her nightie and her feet were bare. She shivered and stared around her at the swirling mists and ghostly vapours.

'Where are we?' she asked.

'We is in Dream Country,' the BFG said. 'This is where all dreams is beginning.'

DREAM-CATCHING

The Big Friendly Giant put the suitcase on the ground. He bent down low so that his enormous face was close to Sophie's. 'From now on, we is keeping as still as winky little micies,' he whispered.

Sophie nodded. The misty vapour swirled around her. It made her cheeks damp and left dewdrops in her hair. The BFG opened the suitcase and took out several empty glass jars. He set them ready on the ground, with their screw tops removed. Then he stood up very straight. His head was now high up in the swirling mist and it kept disappearing, then appearing again. He was holding the long net in his right hand. Sophie, staring upwards, saw through the mist that his colossal ears were beginning to swivel out from his head. They began waving gently to and fro.

Suddenly the BFG pounced. He leaped high in the air and

swung the net through the mist with a great swishing sweep of his arm. 'Got him!' he cried. 'A jar! A jar! Quick quick quick!' Sophie picked up a jar and held it up to him. He grabbed hold of it. He lowered the net. Very carefully he tipped something absolutely invisible from the net into the jar. He dropped the net and swiftly clapped one hand over the jar. 'The top!' he whispered. 'The jar top quick!' Sophie picked up the screw top and handed it to him. He screwed it on tight and the jar was closed. The BFG was very excited. He held the jar close to one ear and listened intently.

'It's a winksquiffler!' he whispered with a thrill in his voice. 'It's . . . it's . . . it's . . . it's even better. It's a phizzwizard! It's a golden phizzwizard!'

Sophie stared at him.

'Oh my, oh my!' he said, holding the jar in front of him. 'This will be giving some little tottler a very happy night when I is blowing it in!'

'Is it really a good one?' Sophie asked.

'A good one?' he cried. 'It's a golden phizzwizard! It is not often I is getting one of these!' He handed the jar to Sophie and said, 'Please be still as a starfish now. I is thinking there may be a whole swarm of phizzwizards up here today. And do kindly stop breathing. You is terribly noisy down there.'

'I haven't moved a muscle,' Sophie said.

'Then don't,' the BFG answered sharply. Once again he stood up tall in the mist, holding his net at the ready. Then came the long silence, the waiting, the listening, and at last, with surprising suddenness came the leap and the swish of the net.

'Another jar!' he cried. 'Quick quick quick!'

When the second dream was safely in the jar and the top was screwed down, the BFG held it to his ear.

'Oh no!' he cried. 'Oh mince my maggots! Oh swipe my swoggles!'

'What's the matter?' Sophie asked.

'It's a trogglehumper!' he shouted. His voice was filled with fury and anguish. 'Oh, save our solos!' he cried. 'Deliver us from weasels! The devil is dancing on my dibbler!'

'What are you talking about?' Sophie said. The BFG was getting more distressed every moment.

'Oh, bash my eyebones!' he cried, waving the jar in the air. 'I come all this way to get lovely golden dreams and what is I catching?'

'What are you catching?' Sophie said.

'I is catching a frightsome trogglehumper!' he cried. 'This is a bad bad dream! It is worse than a bad dream! It is a nightmare!'

'Oh dear,' Sophie said. 'What will you do with that?'

'I is never never letting it go!' the BFG cried. 'If I do, then some poor little tottler will be having the most curdbloodling time! This one is a real kicksy bog thumper! I is exploding it as soon as I get home!'

'Nightmares are horrible,' Sophie said. 'I had one once and I woke up sweating all over.'

'With this one you would be waking up screaming all over!' the BFG said. 'This one would make your teeth stand on end! If this one got into you, your blood would be freezing to icicles and your skin would go creeping across the floor!'

'Is it as bad as that?'

'It's worse!' cried the BFG. 'This is a real whoppsy grobswitcher!'

'You said it was a trogglehumper,' Sophie told him.

'It is a trogglehumper!' cried the exasperated BFG. 'But it is also a bogthumper and a grobswitcher! It is all three riddled into one! Oh, I is so glad I is clutching it tight. Ah, you wicked beastie, you!' he cried, holding up the jar and staring into it. 'Never more is you going to be bunkdoodling the poor little human-beaney tottlers!'

THE EDGE OF THE *Map*

Written and illustrated by
JAMIE LITTLER

'Today is the day you begin your journey towards adulthood. Today is the day you embark upon your Proving!' For the last ten minutes the Star Seer, a master navigator, had been giving what the little girl suspected was a very rousing speech, but she'd barely heard a word of it. She'd been far too busy struggling to keep her breakfast down, which wasn't made any easier by the fact that her heart was thumping against her ribcage like a demented drummer. 'When you return,' the Star Seer continued, 'you will have proven your worth, and will be welcomed back as true Drifters – the bravest explorers the world has ever seen!'

When you return, the little girl thought. *More like if.* She grasped her folded kite tightly against her chest so that the wind wouldn't tear it from her arms. This kite would lead her Ice Cutter snowboard across the frozen land, away from everything she knew. The girl had been looking forward to the Proving all her life, but now that the day had come she found herself wishing she could just carry on with her explorer lessons, as though nothing was changing at all. She knew the Proving was incredibly dangerous. Some children didn't make it back at all. But it was tradition. It was just how things were, how they'd always been. When Drifter children reached ten winters, they had to leave the safety of the Convoy, a fleet of large, roaming, enjin-powered sleighs, on a quest to discover uncharted land and mark it upon the map.

That was all well and good.

Fun, even, maybe.

But when you add in a dangerous world, endlessly sprawling and unforgiving, and the tiny fact that it was infested with gigantic Leviathan monsters that wanted to devour you . . . well.

It dampened one's enthusiasm somewhat.

The little girl looked across at the other children who were lined up beside her on the edge of the sleigh's main deck, the frozen landscape rushing past, blue-purple in the chill morning light. They also looked tense, cloaks thrashing about in the air, grasping their kites like they would their mothers. Their knees knocked together despite their efforts to look brave. Their boots were locked into their Ice Cutter boards, making their trembling legs all the more obvious. She saw someone barfing for the second time that morning. But the girl found relief in their nerves.

Least I'm not the only one.

She gazed out at the Convoy that ran alongside them – the vessels the girl had called home her entire life, twisting and turning across the land like a shoal of fish. It was an incredible sight. One she would miss. For the first time ever, she'd have to leave it behind.

All on her own.

And yet, this wasn't what was bothering her. Not really.

The little girl let out a long, shuddering breath. The Star Seer was still banging on about how important the day was. She gazed over her shoulder at the crowd of people who had come to bid the children farewell. Families and friends, both pride and worry etched on to their faces. The girl spotted her older brother and sister, who made grotesque faces at her the moment she caught their eyes. They'd already completed their Provings and had been boasting about it ever since. She'd been so looking forward to showing them up when she did hers, but now she found herself wishing she'd asked them for advice.

They continued to stick their tongues out, their eyes boggling.

On second thoughts, maybe she didn't want advice from those two. She returned a grotesque face of her own, one she had dubbed 'the Creature of a Hundred Chins'.

Her pa stood behind her gurning siblings. Usually so strong and brave, he now looked fragile and afraid, his lips quivering, eyes shining with worry.

'My baby, my poor baby girl . . . all by herself . . .' Then he buried his head in her ma's shoulder, bawling his eyes out and sniffling.

'Don't you worry, she's a big girl now,' her ma assured him, patting his head. 'She can take care of herself.'

Most children would've taken comfort from these words, maybe even pride. But not this one. This was exactly the reason why the girl's limbs trembled, her heart raced and her breaths came short and fast. Her ma had been all smiles and support, as always. But she seemed about as concerned for the little girl's wellbeing as if she were just taking a lovely stroll across the deck, and wasn't, in fact, about to embark on a potentially life-threatening journey that could take years to complete, if she managed it at all.

The girl's ma was a legend among their people. She was famous for having completed her Proving in record-breaking time, and she'd only been eight winters old when she'd done it! Since then, she'd charted more of the world than any other Drifter in living memory, with more daring deeds and courageous journeys than most would even dream of.

But what if I'm not as good? the girl worried. *What if I'm . . . rubbish, or . . . or I don't discover any place new?* She gulped, her spit sour. *What if I let her down? She'll be humiliated!* The girl looked to her ma for any sign of doubt or concern, anything that showed she didn't expect the world from her daughter. But she simply gave her a calm smile, the briefest nod of her head.

'You've got this,' she mouthed.

I don't got this, I don't got this, the girl panicked.

'And now, children of the Convoy, after my brief words of encouragement,' the Star Seer announced, still yammering on, 'it is time for you to depart!'

The line of children tensed as one. The little girl felt her throat tighten as adrenaline pumped through her veins. 'May the stars guide your way and your compass point you true. Let the Proving begin!'

The children released their kites, frames snapping open and skin sails catching the gusting wind. Gripping the bridles that trailed from the kites, the children flew off the deck, one after the other. The girl left her belly behind, her long, half-shaved hair whipping behind her as she flew through the air. She stole one last glance at the sleigh behind her.

Time seemed to slow for a moment, or perhaps it was for an age.

Because there, amid the cheers of support and sorrow from the watching crowd, the girl saw it.

Her ma was holding her hands to her mouth with worry.

And was it the girl's imagination, or had her pa grasped her ma's shoulder even tighter, to help ease her fears, to reassure her that everything would be OK?

The sight set the girl's heart alight.

She bent her knees, bracing for the impact as the ground raced towards her. In a spray of powdery snow, her Ice Cutter hit the ice, and her kite pulled her along the landscape at breakneck speed. She laughed at the thrill of it, weaving in and out of the other children, her heart singing. Her ma was worried! She'd been acting calm for her sake, probably hoping it'd make the whole thing easier.

'Eat my snow!' Astra, one of the other children, shouted. 'I'll beat all of ya!'

'A race?' The little girl laughed. 'Please, give me a real challenge!' She yanked on the bridle, adjusting her kite as she sped across the snow, leaving the Convoy, her family, her home, behind.

But it didn't matter. Not any more.

I'll prove to Ma she ent got a reason to worry. I'll prove that I'm worthy of her legend! The girl grinned, her brows narrowing with determination. *My name's Lunah. You probably ent heard of me yet, but you will.*

You can bet you will.

LITTLE BADMAN'S
Big Dream

WRITTEN BY HUMZA ARSHAD
& HENRY WHITE
Illustrated by Aleksei Bitskoff

Let me get straight to the point, yeah? You know that story about the guy who dreamed he was munching on the world's biggest marshmallow, then woke up to find he'd eaten his pillow? Well, that guy ain't got nothing on me. My dreams have been crazy lately.

I'm Humza by the way. But you can call me Little Badman – part-time rapper, full-time hero. It's just that no one else seems to know it but me. How many times has a kid got to save the world before he gets some credit around here?!

Anyway, just last week I was having this crazy dream that I was being chased around the neighbourhood by zombies. I was running about, climbing and jumping all over the place. Really putting my ninja skills to good use (and, yeah, I got some sick ninja skills in my dreams, so don't question it!).

But it turns out, everything I was doing in the dream I was actually doing in real life. When I was climbing over a big old army truck in the dream, I was really climbing over my dad's garden shed. When I was karate kicking a zombie, turns out I was karate kicking my neighbour, Mr Akintunde. He's, like, 170 years old and barely managed to get out of the way in time. But you can see why I mistook him for a zombie. He's basically made out of dead skin and ear hair.

So there I was, running through town like a crazy guy. Rolling, leaping, ducking, diving. There's CCTV footage of me shaking a stick at a bunch of confused geese in the park around 10 p.m. That's dangerous stuff, you know. Seriously! You ever been pecked by a goose? Those guys'll take your arm off!

Anyway, turns out CCTV cameras all over Eggington were picking up other kids doing the same kinda thing. At that very second my best friend Umer was having a dream about rounding up unicorns. He'd climbed out of his bedroom window and somehow managed to pick up three sausage dogs and a labradoodle. He had them all on a bit of washing line and was running through the neighbourhood looking for more. And the weird thing was, he and I were headed in the exact same direction. Towards the old abandoned ice rink on Marble Lane. And it wasn't just us ...

Wendy Wang showed up dragging this huge bush behind her. Apparently she thought it was the *Titanic* and she'd rescued everyone by pulling it ashore. Jamal Jones appeared wearing a potato sack instead of pyjamas. Iqbal Kota was covered from head to toe in mud (at least I hope it was mud). Pretty soon, every single kid from my class was there, right in the centre of that dirty old ice rink. And then – snap – we all woke up at the same time ...

'What's going on?' I said to Umer and his dogs. 'Where'd all the zombies go?'

'I've no idea what you're talking about,' replied Umer, 'but I think there's something wrong with my unicorns.'

I didn't even bother trying to figure out what that meant. Everyone was talking at the same time and no one had a clue where they were or why they'd ended up there.

But then I spotted it. Every single kid was carrying something. Along with their bushes and dogs and sticks and whatever – each kid had the very same item under one arm. A copy of that month's book from English class – *The Whispered Word*. It was about some girl who got captured by this horrible circus owner and was forced to work there forever.

I'd found it kind of frustrating cos the ending never tells

you if she escapes or not. My teacher said that's on purpose. He said the author lets you make up your own ending. But that can't be right! I once had to leave the cinema for a wee during the end of *Spider-Man*, and missed the whole last fight. That didn't make it a better film! That just made me regret drinking so much Pepsi.

Anyway, point is, every kid in my class was carrying a copy of *The Whispered Word*. And when I looked down, so was I . . .

As soon as everyone realized how late it was, they all started running off home. Fair enough – if my dad caught me out at this hour he'd force-feed me my own trainers. I was going the same way as Umer and Wendy, so we all ran back together.

'I think the author's trying to tell us something,' said Wendy, as we hurried towards home.

'Me too!' I replied. 'There's something about that book and the ice rink. They must be connected somehow.'

'Probably those downward sentences,' said Umer matter-of-factly.

'What downward sentences?' I asked.

'Well, the book's full of normal sentences going across the page, right? But then there's also the downward ones, running from top to bottom on the left-hand side.'

Wendy opened her copy of the book and, sure enough, there they were! Sentences running down the left-hand side of every single page!

'He's right!' cried Wendy. 'It's an acrostic!'

'A what?' I asked.

'That's when you make the first letter of each sentence form a new sentence running vertically down the page,' she explained. 'You can hide messages there, right in plain sight!'

'How the hell did you spot that, man?' I asked Umer.

'Dunno. I was trying to read but I just kept daydreaming about whether cats have armpits or legpits. That's when my eyes started wandering up and down the page. I suddenly realized I was looking at words.'

'We've got to work it out!' I said, as we rounded the corner, back on to my street. 'Something in that book is making the kids who read it show up at the ice rink. We've got to figure out why.'

The next day at break time we started to copy out every single one of the acrostic words. Every page of the book held part of the secret message. Once we had them written down, we began breaking them into sentences. It didn't take long to discover the author's message:

Dear reader, if you are seeing this, then you have cracked my dream code. Now you must return to that place and dig. Dig deep and you will find the answer to this riddle. Dig deep. Dig. Dig. Dig.

There was a secret buried beneath that old ice rink. And we were gonna dig it up . . .

After school we grabbed a spade from my dad's shed and headed to the ice rink. For two hours straight, we dug. And then, with a loud clang, we hit something hard. We scraped back the dirt to look at what we'd found. And there it was – a rusty metal chest.

'You ready?' I said, once we'd got it out on to the rink.

The others only nodded. As I opened the lid, the hinges screeched, echoing around the empty building like some shrieking monster. But when I looked in, there was nothing but paper.

'What is it?' asked Wendy, as I lifted out the pages.

'I think it's another chapter,' I replied. 'It's the real ending of *The Whispered Word*.'

'What do you think happens in the story?' Wendy asked.

'I think she escapes,' said Umer. 'She gets away from the circus owner and goes home to her parents.'

'I think she gets him arrested and takes over the circus,' suggested Wendy.

'Nah, I think she feeds him to the circus bear,' I said. 'Then she becomes a fighter pilot or a vampire.'

But we had the real answers right there in front of us. So, in silence, the three of us sat there, reading the final secret chapter of *The Whispered Word*. And you know what? All the answers to all our questions were there. What really happened to the hero? Did the evil circus owner get what he deserved? Was there a happy ending?

When we were finished, no one said a word. On the final page, under the printed text, there was a handwritten message:

Now, are you glad you know the ending, or did you prefer your own?

No one spoke. We placed the pages back in the box, placed the box back in the ground, and covered it over with dirt. And you know what, not one of us ever told a soul about what we'd found that afternoon.

You see, it turns out that the author was trying to tell us something. Sometimes the answers are best left to your imagination. Not everything needs to be explained, especially if you've enjoyed the ride. Sometimes the mystery is better than the reveal. Sometimes the stories you dream up are the best stories of them all.

Except, of course, when it comes to Spider-Man movies. Don't make the mistake I made. Have a wee before you go in! I still have no idea how they beat that stupid vulture guy!

My big dream is to dive into a candy land. It would have trees as candy sticks, tulips made of cookies. The grass would be Haribo sweets and the concrete would be chocolate bars. Plastic bags would be made out of biscuits, paper would be candyfloss. Everybody would enjoy my creation. You'd never need to buy sweets again. There would still be healthy foods but there would be more unhealthy foods.

It all started yesterday afternoon when I went to the shops and spent hundreds of pounds on sweets. So I went into my garden and replaced the tulips with cookies, the grass with sweets, and the concrete with chocolate. It took a while to take the trees down – they're nearly all replaced with candy sticks.

My candy land became famous! People came into my candy land and started to eat my surroundings. I had to carry on buying supplies until I ran out of money and people ate everything else that was left. No more candy land.

Suddenly I woke up and it was all a dream.

JAYDEN, AGE 10, CASTLECOMBE PRIMARY SCHOOL

A Curious ENCOUNTER

FROM

THE BORROWERS

WRITTEN BY MARY NORTON

Illustrated by Siân Bailey

It was an eye. Or it looked like an eye. Clear and bright like the colour of the sky. An eye like her own but enormous. A glaring eye. Breathless with fear, she sat up. And the eye blinked. A great fringe of lashes came curving down and flew up again out of sight. Cautiously, Arrietty moved her legs: she would slide noiselessly in among the grass stems and slither away down the bank.

'Don't move!' said a voice, and the voice, like the eye, was enormous but somehow hushed – and hoarse like a surge of wind through the grating on a stormy night in March.

Arrietty froze. 'So this is it,' she thought, 'the worst and most terrible thing of all: I have been "seen"! Whatever happened to

Eggletina will now, almost certainly, happen to me!'

There was a pause and Arrietty, her heart pounding in her ears, heard the breath again drawn swiftly into the vast lungs. 'Or,' said the voice, whispering still, 'I shall hit you with my ash stick.'

Suddenly Arrietty became calm. 'Why?' she asked. How strange her own voice sounded! Crystal thin and harebell clear, it tinkled on the air.

'In case,' came the surprised whisper at last, 'you ran towards me, quickly, through the grass . . . in case,' it went on, trembling a little, 'you scrabbled at me with your nasty little hands.'

Arrietty stared at the eye; she held herself quite still. 'Why?' she asked again, and again the word tinkled – icy cold it sounded this time, and needle sharp.

'Things do,' said the voice. 'I've seen them. In India.'

Arrietty thought of her *Gazetteer of the World*. 'You're not in India now,' she pointed out.

'Did you come out of the house?'

'Yes,' said Arrietty.

'From whereabouts in the house?'

Arrietty stared at the eye. 'I'm not going to tell you,' she said at last bravely.

'Then I'll hit you with my ash stick!'

'All right,' said Arrietty, 'hit me!'

'I'll pick you up and break you in half!'

Arrietty stood up. 'All right,' she said and took two paces forward.

There was a sharp gasp and an earthquake in the grass: he spun away from her and sat up, a great mountain in a green jersey. He had fair, straight hair and golden eyelashes. 'Stay where you are!' he cried.

Arrietty stared up at him. So this was 'the boy'! Breathless, she felt, and light with fear. 'I guessed you were about nine,' she gasped after a moment.

He flushed. 'Well, you're wrong, I'm ten.' He looked down at her, breathing deeply. 'How old are you?'

'Fourteen,' said Arrietty. 'Next June,' she added, watching him.

There was silence while Arrietty waited, trembling a little.

'Can you read?' the boy said at last.

'Of course,' said Arrietty. 'Can't you?'

'No,' he stammered. 'I mean – yes. I mean I've just come from India.'

'What's that got to do with it?' asked Arrietty.

'Well, if you're born in India, you're bilingual. And if you're bilingual, you can't read. Not so well.'

Arrietty stared up at him: 'What a monster,' she thought, 'dark against the sky.'

'Do you grow out of it?' she asked.

He moved a little and she felt the cold flick of his shadow.

'Oh yes,' he said, 'it wears off. My sisters were bilingual; now they aren't a bit. They could read any of those books upstairs in the schoolroom.'

'So could I,' said Arrietty quickly, 'if someone could hold them, and turn the pages. I'm not a bit bilingual. I can read anything.'

'Could you read out loud?'

'Of course,' said Arrietty.

'Would you wait here while I run upstairs and get a book now?'

'Well,' said Arrietty; she was longing to show off; then a startled look came into her eyes. 'Oh –' she faltered.

'What's the matter?' The boy was standing up now. He towered above her.

'How many doors are there to this house?' She squinted up at him against the bright sunlight. He dropped on one knee.

'Doors?' he said. 'Outside doors?'

'Yes.'

'Well, there's the front door, the back door, the gun-room door, the kitchen door, the scullery door . . . and the French windows in the drawing-room.'

'Well, you see,' said Arrietty, 'my father's in the hall, by the front door, working. He . . . he wouldn't want to be disturbed.'

'Working?' said the boy. 'What at?'

'Getting material,' said Arrietty, 'for a scrubbing-brush.'

'Then I'll go in the side door.' He began to move away but turned suddenly and came back to her. He stood a moment, as though embarrassed, and then he said: 'Can you fly?'

'No,' said Arrietty, surprised; 'can you?'

His face became even redder. 'Of course not,' he said angrily; 'I'm not a fairy!'

'Well, nor am I,' said Arrietty, 'nor is anybody. I don't believe in them.'

He looked at her strangely. 'You don't believe in them?'

'No,' said Arrietty; 'do you?'

'Of course not!'

'Really,' she thought, 'he is a very angry kind of boy'. 'My mother believes in them,' she said, trying to appease him. 'She thinks she saw one once. It was when she was a girl and lived with her parents behind the sand pile in the potting-shed.'

He squatted down on his heels and she felt his breath on her face. 'What was it like?' he asked.

'About the size of a glow-worm with wings like a butterfly. And it had a tiny little face, she said, all alight and moving like sparks and tiny moving hands. Its face was changing all the time, she said, smiling and sort of shimmering. It seemed to be talking, she said, very quickly – but you couldn't hear a word.'

'Oh,' said the boy, interested. After a moment he asked: 'Where did it go?'

'It just went,' said Arrietty. 'When my mother saw it, it seemed to be caught in a cobweb. It was dark at the time. About five o'clock on a winter's evening. After tea.'

'Oh,' he said again and picked up two petals of cherry-blossom which he folded together like a sandwich and ate slowly. 'Supposing,' he said, staring past her at the wall of the house, 'you saw a little man, about as tall as a pencil, with a blue patch on his trousers, half-way up a window curtain, carrying a doll's tea-cup – would you say it was a fairy?'

'No,' said Arrietty, 'I'd say it was my father.'

'Oh,' said the boy, thinking this out, 'does your father have a blue patch on his trousers?'

'Not on his best trousers. He does on his borrowing ones.'

'Oh,' said the boy again. He seemed to find it a safe sound, as lawyers do. 'Are there many people like you?'

'No,' said Arrietty. 'None. We're all different.'

'I mean as small as you?'

Arrietty laughed. 'Oh, don't be silly!' she said. 'Surely you don't think there are many people in the world your size?'

'There are more my size than yours,' he retorted.

'Honestly –' began Arrietty helplessly and laughed again. 'Do you really think – I mean, whatever sort of a world would it be? Those great chairs . . . I've seen them. Fancy if you had to make chairs that size for everyone? And the stuff for their clothes . . . miles and miles of it . . . tents of it . . . and the sewing! And their great houses, reaching up so you can hardly see the ceilings . . . their great beds . . . the food they eat . . . great, smoking mountains of it, huge bogs of stew and soup and stuff.'

'Don't you eat soup?' asked the boy.

'Of course we do,' laughed Arrietty. 'My father had an uncle who had a little boat which he rowed round in the stock-pot picking up flotsam and jetsam. He did bottom-fishing too for bits of marrow until the cook got suspicious through finding bent pins in the soup. Once he was nearly shipwrecked on a chunk of submerged shin-bone. He lost his oars and the boat sprang a leak but he flung a line over the pot handle and pulled himself alongside the rim. But all that stock – fathoms of it! And the size of the stock-pot! I mean, there wouldn't be enough stuff in the world to go round after a bit! That's why my father says it's a good thing they're dying out . . . just a few, my father says, that's all we need – to keep us. Otherwise, he says, the whole thing gets' – Arrietty hesitated, trying to remember the word – 'exaggerated, he says –'

'What do you mean,' asked the boy, '"to keep us"?'

Shy Bairns
GET NOWT

WRITTEN BY BETH LINCOLN

Illustrated by Renia Metallinou

The shop appeared overnight, squeezing itself in next to Shoe Palace, where Mags's big sister used to work. It had a bright purple sign that said RUBBLE'S, and lanterns over the door cupping pink flames. A tattered poster in the window said CROW'S FEET: BUY TWO, GET ONE FREE! All the other shops on the high street were closed down, packed up and soaped over – Rubble's stuck out like a swollen purple thumb.

Mags munched her sweets and eyed the new shop. It was probably dodgy, but then Mags's mam always said: *Shy bairns get nowt.* Her mam was rarely wrong.

She went in. A bell chimed.

Inside, the dust was thick enough to shovel. The items on the shelves had labels like PICKLED SPITE and ASSORTED GIZZARDS and CANNED COLLYWOBBLES, and half of them were out of date.

A barrel of eyes watched Mags move around the shop.

She poked a bottle, and something in it wriggled.

'Oi!'

She almost knocked the bottle off the shelf. Behind the counter was a being, knobbled and knotted like a toad, with a wide mouth and beady black eyes. He was wearing an apron.

Now, Mags was sharp, and her nan was Scottish, and she'd been raised on tales of the Wee Folk. She knew a fairy shop when she saw one.

The troll behind the counter – his name tag said RUBBLE – tapped a glowing pink crystal by the till. 'This is *supposed* to keep you humans out,' he grumbled. Then he spotted the sweet packet in her hand. 'Them's fairy sweets!' he rumbled. 'In fact, them's stolen fairy sweets! No wonder you could get in!'

Mags tried to argue that she'd found the sweets on a park bench (this was true, and there's a lesson there) but the troll was having none of it. When Mags tried to pay, he ate the fiver she gave him.

'Only take gold,' he said. 'And if you can't pay, you work.' He tossed an apron at her.

Mags tried to leave, but the doorknob burned at her touch.

'Your shift's not over,' growled Rubble.

For three hours Mags swept, and stacked shelves, and served customers. It was tiring work.

'Don't worry, little thief,' chuckled the troll. 'Only nine years, eleven months, thirty days and twenty-one hours to go!'

Mags nearly collapsed. Ten years! She'd be ancient by then. She'd be her sister's age.

That gave her an idea. Mags was sharp, and she'd noticed the shop was very, very quiet.

'If only my sister Alice was here,' she sighed. 'She's the best Sales Assistant – er, I mean, Sales Witch – in the county.'

Rubble pretended not to listen, but one ear twitched.

Shy bairns get nowt, thought Mags.

'I bet she could double your gold in a single day.'

Mags's nan had always said the Wee Folk loved to gamble. Her nan, like her mam, was rarely wrong.

'A Sales Witch, eh? You're on,' said Rubble. 'But if you lose – I'll double your shift.'

Now, however sharp Mags was, Alice was just as sharp, with an extra ten years' practice. When she arrived, she looked about the shop and tutted.

'The state of this,' she said scornfully. 'You're lucky I'm here.'

'Who d'you think you are?' spluttered Rubble.

Alice fixed him with a look. 'I'm the best Sales Witch in the county.'

She got to work. She tore down the peeling posters, rearranged the shelves and shovelled away the dust. She put in a nice window display. She wielded her red pen like a wand, slashing and raising prices.

But most importantly, when Rubble's back was turned, she and Mags smashed the crystal behind the counter.

Customers began to trickle in, and though some of them were Rubble's usual sort – boggarts, pixies, redcaps and the like – for the first time there were a few humans as well.

'The high street's been falling apart for years,' said old Mrs Aiken. 'A quirky shop

like this is just what we need!' She bought an energy potion with one of her gold earrings and danced out of the shop.

Mr Maan bought a ball of organic yeti wool. 'I can knit a gorgeous jumper with this,' he said, and handed over his signet ring.

By the end of the day, gold was spilling out of the till and on to the floor. Rubble had never seen such powerful magic. He wanted to hire Alice on the spot.

'Hang on,' said Alice. 'I'm not working for more than eight hours a day. No weekends. And I want decent wages.'

Rubble smiled greedily. 'I'll pay you as much gold as you can fit in one pocket of your apron. Per week.'

Mags stifled a gasp, but Alice shook her head. 'Make that two pockets, and you've got a deal.'

She even got Rubble to give her a week's pay in advance. She and Mags jingled their way back up the high street.

'It's like Mam always says,' said Alice, and she and Mags chorused: 'Shy bairns get nowt!'

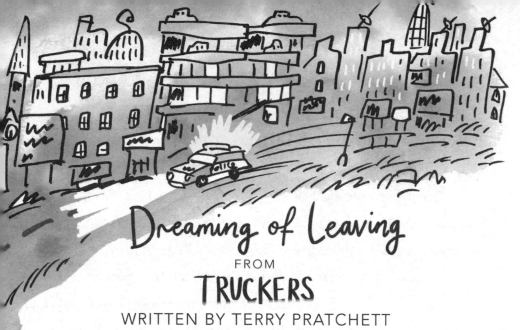

Dreaming of Leaving

FROM

TRUCKERS

WRITTEN BY TERRY PRATCHETT

Illustrated by Mark Beech

There had been plenty of them, in the days when it didn't seem to rain so much. Masklin could remember at least forty. But then the motorway had come; the stream was put in pipes underground, and the nearest hedges were grubbed up. Nomes had always lived in the corners of the world, and suddenly there weren't too many corners any more.

The numbers started going down. A lot of this was due to natural causes, and when you're four inches high natural causes can be anything with teeth and speed and hunger. Then Pyrrince, who was by way of being the most adventurous, led a desperate expedition *across the carriageway* one night, to investigate the woods on the other side. They never came back. Some said it was hawks, some said it was a lorry. Some even said they'd made it halfway and were marooned on the central reservation between endless swishing lines of cars.

Then the cafe had been built, a little further along the road. It had been a sort of improvement. It depended how you looked at it. If cold leftover chips and scraps of grey chicken were food, then there was suddenly enough for everyone.

And then it was spring, and Masklin looked around and found that there were just ten of them left, and eight of those were too old to get about much. Old Torrit was nearly ten.

It had been a dreadful summer. Grimma organized those who could still get about into midnight raids on the litter-bins, and Masklin tried to hunt.

Hunting by yourself was like dying a bit at a time. Most of the things you were hunting were also hunting *you*. And even if you were lucky and made a kill, how did you get it home? It had taken two days with the rat, including sitting out at night to fight off other creatures. Ten strong hunters could do anything – rob bees' nests, trap mice, catch moles, *anything* – but one hunter by himself, with no one to watch his back in the long grass, was simply the next meal for everything with talons and claws.

To get enough to eat, you needed lots of healthy hunters.

But to get lots of healthy hunters, you needed enough to eat.

'It'll be all right in the autumn,' said Grimma, bandaging his arm where a stoat had caught it. 'There'll be mushrooms and berries and nuts and everything.'

Well, there hadn't been any mushrooms and it rained so much that most of the berries rotted before they ripened. There were plenty of nuts, though. The nearest hazel tree was half a day's journey away. Masklin could carry a dozen nuts if he smashed them out of their shells and dragged them back in a paper bag from the bin. It took a whole day to do it, risking hawks all the way, and it was just enough food for a day as well.

And then the back of the burrow fell in, because of all the rain. It was almost pleasant to get out, then. It was better than listening to the grumbling about him not doing essential repairs. Oh, and there was the fire. You needed a fire at the burrow mouth; both for cooking and for keeping away night prowlers.

Granny Morkie went to sleep one day and let it go out. Even she had the decency to be embarrassed.

When Masklin came back that night he looked at the heap of dead ashes for a long time and then stuck his spear in the ground and burst out laughing, and went on laughing until he started to cry. He couldn't face the rest of them. He had to go and sit outside where, presently, Grimma brought him a shellful of nettle tea. *Cold* nettle tea.

'They're all very upset about it,' she volunteered.

Masklin gave a hollow laugh. 'Oh, yes, I can tell,' he said, 'I've heard them. "You ought to bring back another fag-end, boy, I'm right out of tobacco," and "We never have fish these days, you might find the time to go down to the river," and "Self, self, self, that's all you young people think about, in my day—"'

Grimma sighed. 'They do their best,' she said. 'It's just that they don't realize. There were hundreds of us when they were young.'

'It's going to take *days* to get that fire lit,' said Masklin. They had a spectacle lens; it needed a very sunny day to work.

He poked aimlessly in the mud by his feet.

'I've had enough,' he said quietly. 'I'm going to leave.'

'But we need you!'

'I need me too. I mean, what kind of life is this?'

'But they'll die if you go away!'

'They'll die anyway,' said Masklin.

'That's a wicked thing to say!'

'Well, it's true. Everyone dies anyway. *We'll* die anyway. Look at you. You spend your whole time washing and tidying up and cooking and chasing after them. You're nearly three! It's about time you had a life of your own.'

'Granny Morkie was very kind to me when I was small,' said Grimma defensively. 'You'll be old one day.'

'You think? And who will be working their fingers to the bone to look after me?'

Masklin found himself getting angrier and angrier. He was certain he was in the right. But it *felt* as if he was in the wrong, which made it worse.

He'd thought about this for a long time, and it had always left him feeling angry and awkward. All the clever ones and the bold ones and the brave ones had gone long ago, one way or the other. Good old Masklin, they'd said, stout chap, you look after the old folk and we'll be back before you know it, just as soon as we've found a better place. Every time good old Masklin thought about this he got indignant with them for going and with himself for staying. He always gave in, that was his trouble. He knew it. Whatever he promised himself at the start, he always took the way of least resistance.

Grimma was glaring at him.

He shrugged.

'All right, all right, so they can come with us,' he said.

'You know they won't go,' she said. 'They're too old. They all grew up round here. They like it here.'

'They like it here when there's us around to wait on them,' muttered Masklin.

They left it at that. There were nuts for dinner. Masklin's had a maggot in it.

He went out afterwards and sat at the top of the bank with his chin in his hands, watching the motorway again.

It was a stream of red and white lights. There were humans inside those boxes, going about whatever mysterious business humans spent their time on. They were always in a hurry to get to it, whatever it was.

He was prepared to bet they didn't eat rat. Humans had it

really easy. They were big and slow, but they didn't have to live in damp burrows waiting for daft old women to let the fire go out. They never had maggots in their tea. They went wherever they wanted and they did whatever they liked. The whole world belonged to them.

And all night long they drove up and down in these little lorries with lights on. Didn't they ever go to sleep? There must be hundreds of them.

He'd dreamed of leaving on a lorry. They often stopped at the cafe. It would be easy – well, fairly easy – to find a way onto one. They were clean and shiny, they had to go somewhere better than this. And after all, what was the alternative? They'd never see winter through, here, and setting out across the fields with the bad weather coming on didn't bear thinking about.

Of course, he'd never do it. You never actually did it, in the end. You just dreamed about following those swishing lights.

King OF THE World

WRITTEN BY CHARLIE HIGSON
Illustrated by Fred Blunt

One night Bill dreamed that he was King of the World – and the next day he was.

This is how it happened.

It was a Sunday, and Bill had been playing a game on his phone for hours. In the end his mum got so fed up, she took his phone away from him.

'What *is* that silly game you play all the time anyway?' she said, in the voice she used when she was tired and cross.

'It's called *King of the World*,' said Bill, in the voice he used when he was excited about something. 'You have to beat all the other players and become King of the World: first you have to build a town, then you have to build farms and mines with farmers and miners, and woodcutters to cut down trees, and the more gold you get, the more you can upgrade your town until you get a barracks, and then you make soldiers and you attack other towns and steal their gold and use it to make your town bigger, and then you can invade more and more countries until you become King of the World . . .'

But his mum hadn't been listening. She locked his phone in a drawer.

'Mu-um,' said Bill.

'Bed,' she said.

When Bill got into bed and closed his eyes, he could still see the little people in the game running around in his head, and for a long while he couldn't get to sleep.

So he lay there thinking about the game and how he could get better at it. Because, even though he played it whenever he could, and was really quite good at it, he'd never actually won it and become King of the World. Not once.

He figured that if he could just spend more time playing the game, he'd eventually crack it.

When at last he went to sleep, Bill dreamed that he was playing the game, and he did so well that he won and everyone said he was cool and should become King of the Actual, Real World, and they gave him a crown and everything.

When Bill's mum came in to wake him up for school, he told her all about his dream.

'It was brilliant being King of the World,' he said. 'I could do whatever I liked and everyone had to obey me. Even you.'

'You'll never become King of the World,' said his mum, 'so long as you waste all your time playing that stupid game. And I'm not giving your phone back until you can promise me you're going to stop.'

'Mu-um.'

But it turned out that his mum was wrong.

Because, due to a mix-up at the Organization of Fairy Godmothers, Genies, Magic Talking Fish and Leprechauns (known as OOFGGMTFAL for short), the Chief Genie was sent to give Bill an Extra Special Super Powerful Wish – the most powerful wish that OOFGGMTFAL had ever invented. The wish was supposed to have been given to a Swedish schoolgirl with pigtails who wanted to save the planet but it was sent to

Bill instead (as I say, this was because of a mix-up which is far too complicated to go into here, but was basically because OOFGGMTFAL had a new computer system that nobody knew how to work properly).

So, later that day, as Bill was having his tea, there was a puff of smoke and the Chief Genie appeared in his kitchen.

'Bill Barnard,' he said, crossing his arms. 'I am the Chief Genie and I am here to tell you that you have been granted an Extra Special Super Powerful Wish (terms and conditions apply). Now, I want you to think long and hard before you choose your wish, because it's very important. This wish is the most –'

'Great,' said Bill, interrupting him. 'I wish I was King of the World!'

'What? Don't you want to think about it for a bit?' said the Chief Genie, who was a bit miffed. 'You've only got one choice and –'

'No,' said Bill. 'I know what I want.' And that was how he became King of the World.

Now that he'd got his wish, Bill could do whatever he wanted and everyone had to obey him. So he stopped going to school and he sat in his palace playing *King of the World* on his phone all day, and his mum couldn't do anything about it.

But one day Bill's chief adviser came to visit him in the palace. And he brought Bill's mum with him.

'Your majesty,' he said. 'You are King of the World. You can do anything and everything. And you need to do a lot more than just play that game all day. Everything's going wrong. There are wars breaking out that you need to stop. There are diseases that must be cured. People are starving. And Swindon needs a new bus timetable.'

'But I didn't become King of the World so I could do all those things,' said Bill. 'I did it so I could play my game without being bothered all the time.'

'Be that as it may,' said the adviser, 'as King of the World you are responsible for everything and, quite frankly, it's all falling to bits.'

'Don't you care about all the people?' said Bill's mum.

'Mu-um,' said Bill. 'Leave me alone.'

So they left him alone. But Bill, who was actually quite

bored with his game, and still hadn't won, thought and thought and thought about all the problems of the world. And after ten minutes he hadn't even thought about half of them. So he called the young Swedish girl on his phone and asked her if she'd like to be King of the World instead, or maybe Queen. And she said OK, but she'd prefer a gender-neutral title. So she became Ruler of the World, and that was that.

Bill went back to school, and he soon got into football, and that was all he thought about and talked about. So much so that his mum sometimes wished he'd go back to playing games on his phone quietly in the corner.

But one day after school, when he was having his tea and thinking about football, three aliens materialized in his kitchen. They had three arms each, and three legs and three eyes.

'Greetings, Mighty Bill,' said the Chief Alien (who was called Oofggmtfal funnily enough, even though he had nothing to do with the Organization of Fairy Godmothers, Genies, Magic Talking Fish and Leprechauns – it was just a coincidence).

'The Universe is in great danger, but the new computer we've had installed at Intergalactic Headquarters has told us that you, Bill Barnard, can save it! So we hereby announce that you are King of the Universe!'

And Bill didn't know what to do. He really needed some help, so he called out in his loudest voice . . .

'Mu-um!'

When I was 7¾, I had a big dream – I wanted to go into space – and my dream still has a strong hold on me. I still want to get out there. It started with the Moon Landings in 1969: after that the world was abuzz with Moon Madness.

I wanted to walk where Neil Armstrong had walked, and then fly on to the planet inhabited by the Clangers (a family of knitted space creatures from one of my favourite TV shows).

Unfortunately, it seemed like an impossible dream. At school I had undiagnosed dyslexia, and was told that I would be unable to become an astronaut. I was lucky though: I got lots of support at home and was able to study hard and become a space scientist. And I am getting closer to my other dreams too. A special episode of the Clangers was made to celebrate their 50th anniversary, and in the show an astronaut visits their wonderful planet – and that astronaut was me. Impossible dreams can come true. Next stop the Moon!!

DR MAGGIE ADERIN-POCOCK, ASTROPHYSICIST

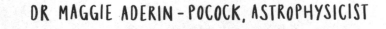

Elephant

WRITTEN BY JEREMY STRONG

Illustrated by Nadia Shireen

E lephant was in the zoo TV room. He was sitting there with the other elephants, watching the British Grand Prix. The cars were loud and Elephant liked that. He made noises down his trunk. **'VROOOOM!'**

Elephant was happy and he sat there dreaming of driving a car himself. When he was in his enclosure at the zoo, if he stood on his back legs and looked over the wall, he could see the road. He would stand there for ages, watching the cars, buses and trucks go backwards and forwards. How he wished he could drive a car!

Then a day came that was very special for Elephant. A truck came to the zoo and it parked RIGHT OUTSIDE Elephant's room. It was big and it was yellow and it had four wheels and a big shovel at the front.

Elephant watched with growing excitement as a man climbed out of the glass cab. You could get in and out of them!

You could sit in them! Elephant murmured dreamily to himself. **'VROOOOM!'**

All day long the yellow truck stayed outside Elephant's room. It scooped up earth in one place and put in another. The man got in and out of his cab several times. One time the man got out, sat on the bucket and ate his packed lunch!

However, by mid-afternoon the yellow truck had gone and Elephant was left dreaming. That very night he woke up and noticed a crack of light round the edge of the door. It hadn't been shut properly. Elephant sniffed around the door with his trunk and soon had it open. He went for a walk. He sniffed at the ground where the yellow truck had been. It smelled of oil and rubber. Elephant gave a sigh of delight. Oil and rubber! His favourite scent. He would have liked to rub it into his armpits – or rather his leg-pits, like deodorant.

Elephant carried on walking and eventually he found himself at the zoo exit. Glory be! The big iron gates were wide open. Obviously nobody thought an elephant would be up and wandering about in the middle of the night. Elephant wandered out on to the street and – oh my gosh and knock me down with a feather – there were cars and vans and even a car transporter!

VROOOOM! Elephant ran towards the empty transporter. The top deck sloped down to the road where it had been unloaded. Elephant climbed up the ramp, right to the top. He plonked himself down and fell asleep.

In the morning the transporter driver came back. He put the car decks back up. He climbed into the cab and drove off. When Elephant woke up he couldn't believe it. He was driving the truck! Well, not exactly driving, but gazing out happily. Every so often he would lift his trunk and hoot.

VROOOOM! PARP-PARP!

If you see an elephant on a car transporter, please don't stop the driver and tell him. Elephant is living the dream.

Caveman Dream
BIG HUGE DREAM

WRITTEN BY SAM COPELAND

Illustrated by Sarah Horne

It was the year 1,000,000 BC, and it was a wet Wednesday afternoon.

The caveboy had been chipping and banging at the stone for days and he had finally done it. At last he had finished!

He ran back to the cave as fast as he could, not feeling the pain of the twigs and sharp rocks under his bare feet.

'Dad!' he shouted. 'Dad! Come quick!'

His dad, muddy-faced and wild of beard, poked his head out of the cave.

'What matter?!' he grunted. 'You fall in mammoth poo again?'

'No! Come and have a look at what I invented!'

'What mean *invented*?'

'It means I thought of something and I made it and I think it's great! Here it is!' the caveboy said, gesturing to his invention.

'What that?'

'I call it a *wheel*!' the boy said proudly.

'It rubbish,' the cavedad replied.

'No! It will be really useful for moving stuff, and maybe we could use it for transport and –'

'It big huge waste of time, that's what is! Why you always dreaming? Stop dreaming and go hunt sabretooth tiger for dinner!'

The caveboy trudged off, deflated.

The boy was not to be kept down for too long, though. A few days later he had another idea. He took two sticks and some tiny bits of bark, and started rubbing the sticks together as fast as he could. For hours and hours he twisted and rubbed the sticks, so that his arms ached and his hands were red raw – until a tiny tendril of smoke appeared. He kept going for hours longer, until finally, when he was about to collapse, the smoke caught the bark, and little licks of fire appeared. He had done it! Fire! This would change everyth–

'WHAT THAT?' his dad screamed suddenly from behind him.

'Dad! I call it *fire*! It will keep us warm during winter and –'

His words were cut off as his dad's great hairy foot began to stamp out the fire.

'Me no like! It look dangerous!'

A moment later it was nothing but ashes – just like the boy's dreams.

'Why you always dreaming, boy? Stop dreaming and go hunt sabretooth tiger for dinner!'

Although devastated, the boy soon pulled himself together. He had another idea.

He found some shells and ground them down into a powder, and then mixed this with water to make a thick paste.

He ran into the cave and started smearing it on the wall.

A while later he called his dad.

He held his dad's hand and proudly showed him the painting on the cave wall.

'What THAT?' his father grunted.

'I call it a *painting*. And it's a picture of you!'

'Me? That no me! Why you give me big nose?'

'Dad, you have a big nose!'

The dad gasped, holding his nose.

'I NO HAVE BIG NOSE!' And he picked up a discarded animal skin and began furiously rubbing the painting off. 'Why you always dreaming, boy? Stop dreaming, stop wasting time and go hunt sabretooth tiger for dinner!'

The caveboy could not stop the tears falling, and he ran out of the cave to hide his sadness.

His father called after him, but the boy didn't stop.

The cavefather looked at the rubbed-out painting, and

remembered the wheel and the fire.

And although cavefather didn't yet have the words to express it, he was feeling bad for crushing his son's dreams.

He had to make it up to caveson.

So he did something he had never done before. He sat down and just thought. He thought as hard as he could.

And then suddenly he had it!

He had an idea!

A few days later, after some searching, cavedad found caveson, still looking sad, sitting on the edge of a small cliff, looking out at the setting sun.

'Son. I sorry. I squash your dreams like delicious bugs we find in cave. So I make present for you so you no sad.'

The boy looked up and his father passed him something. A small black box.

'I dream big HUGE dream,' cavefather said proudly.

'What is it?' the boy asked.

'I call it *compooter*,' said his dad proudly. 'You can look pictures of cute little kittens and send message to friends and watch Netfli–'

The dad gasped as the boy suddenly flung the compooter off the cliff. The smash as it landed was faint.

'Dad,' the boy said, putting his hand on his dad's shoulder. 'Thanks, but I really don't see *compooters* taking off. Maybe in future you should leave the dreaming to me.'

'Yes. You right. Compooter terrible idea.' The dad smiled and rubbed caveson's hair. 'Now, how about we both stop dreaming – let's go hunt sabretooth tiger for dinner. Together.'

And so they strode off into the dying sun, both carrying sharp sticks, bellies rumbling, looking for their dinner.

My big dream is to go back in time to when all the dinosaurs were alive. Yes, I know it's impossible but I always say 'nothing is impossible'. I've always imagined all the humongous creatures that stomped around. Some eating all the leaves on top of the trees and some fighting for their life.

I go to the junkyard every day to find all the pieces I need to make my FABULOUS INVENTION. There were a lot of objects such as piles of discarded metal that could be used to make my invention stay strong. There were colourful wires that were like glowing worms. I would go home day after day with something different.

A few years later, the amazing time-traveller was finally finished. I told my friend Jane all about the invention. She volunteered to try it out. As she stepped in, I pressed the buttons to start it. CHUG! CHUG! CHUG! went the machine. Suddenly, the machine started to malfunction and it said 'NOT WORKING'.

The door opened and no one was there. What had I done?

EILEEN, AGE 10, CASTLECOMBE PRIMARY SCHOOL

'The Very Hungry
Caterpillar story
is about hope.
You, like the
little caterpillar,
will grow up,
unfold your wings
and fly off
into the future.'

WRITTEN AND ILLUSTRATED BY ERIC CARLE
creator of The Very Hungry Caterpillar

The Diary of A YOUNG GIRL

WRITTEN BY ANNE FRANK

Illustrated by Harry Brockway

WEDNESDAY 3 MAY 1944

I've often been down in the dumps, but never desperate. I look upon our life in hiding as an interesting adventure, full of danger and romance, and every privation as an amusing addition to my diary. I've made up my mind to lead a different life from other girls, and not to become an ordinary housewife later on. What I'm experiencing here is a good beginning to an interesting life, and that's the reason – the only reason – why I have to laugh at the humorous side of the most dangerous moments.

I'm young and have many hidden qualities; I'm young and strong and living through a big adventure; I'm right in the middle of it and can't spend all day complaining because it's impossible to have any fun! I'm blessed with many things: happiness, a cheerful disposition and strength. Every day I feel myself maturing, I feel liberation drawing near, I feel the beauty of nature and the goodness of the people around me. Every day I think what a fascinating and amusing adventure this is! With all that, why should I despair?

Yours, Anne M. Frank

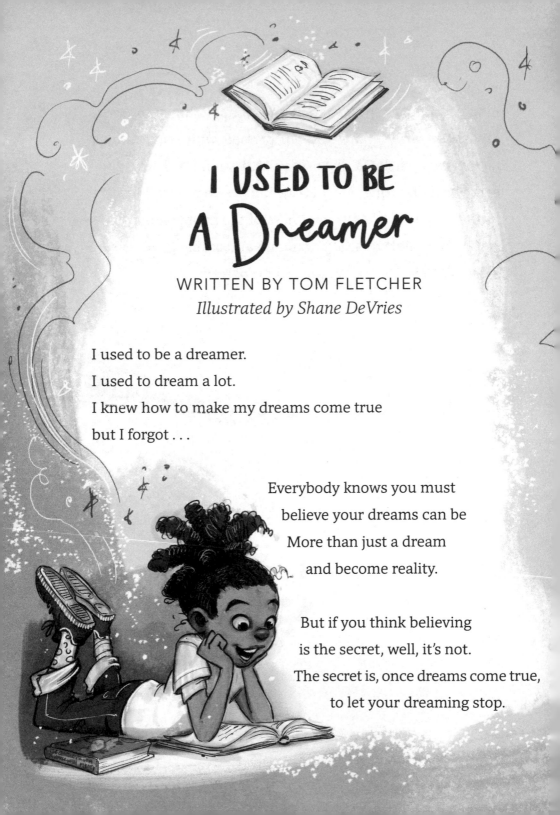

I USED TO BE
A Dreamer

WRITTEN BY TOM FLETCHER
Illustrated by Shane DeVries

I used to be a dreamer.
I used to dream a lot.
I knew how to make my dreams come true
but I forgot . . .

Everybody knows you must
believe your dreams can be
More than just a dream
and become reality.

But if you think believing
is the secret, well, it's not.
The secret is, once dreams come true,
to let your dreaming stop.

I don't mean for forever,
just a while to take it in,
To smell the roses, so they say,
Before you dream again.

For only when you stop
And take a look at what you have
You might find you've already got
the thing you wish you had.

Sure you can go on dreaming
till the day that you are old,
Always striving for perfection,
Never settling for gold,
Always pushing past the limit,
Going over the threshold,
Getting everything you want,
Then you want it sevenfold,

But why cook the perfect dinner
and then let the food get cold?

If you're thinking of dessert
Through your appetizer, then you
Never taste what's in your mouth
With your eyes upon the menu.

Eat it while it's nice and hot –
it doesn't last for long.
Dream again tomorrow.
You'll put the stove back on.

Or what's the point in wishing up
these dreams inside your head?
They'll pass you by so quickly
If you stay one dream ahead.

Trust me, that's what I did.
I was always hoping, wishing.
I caught the perfect catch,
then thought,
I might just keep on fishing.

And sure enough, behind my back,
That dream just slipped away,
And now, I hope, and wish, and pray
I'll dream it back someday.

So, dream big, kid,
For life gives back exactly what you give it.
Just make sure when your dream comes true
You stop a while
to live it.

A DREAM OF
Green AND Silver

WRITTEN BY CATHY CASSIDY

Illustrated by Shaw Davidson

The stream runs along the edge of the playing field at Silverbrook Primary, and it's my favourite place to sit and dream. It's quiet and peaceful, somewhere to be alone, or to make daisy chains and pick blackberries with friends. In the summer you can slip your shoes and socks off and let the cold water rush over your toes, and the jolt of it makes you feel more alive than anything else in the world.

Well, it used to be that way.

Lately, the water has been looking brown and brackish, brightened only by the Coke cans and crisp packets bobbing on

the surface. A pink plastic doll's pram dangles from the hedge.

Even so, finding the blackbird is a shock. It's so still and small and silent, lying on the grass beside the stream, its feathers soft and glossy, as though it might wake up and fly away at any moment. It won't, though. It won't ever fly again. A tangle of blue plastic twine is wrapped round its legs, and wisps of blue stick out of its tiny yellow beak – it has tried to peck through the twine, free itself.

It's the same twine we use in the school garden to tie the runner beans to the bamboo canes . . . some of it must have been dropped and blown over here. It's our fault the blackbird is dead. I find a sharp stone and dig a hole in the mud, place the bird inside and cover it with soil and stones.

Later, in class, I paint a picture where the stream sparkles silver again and the grass is green and littered with daisies. The blackbird soars above it all, wings spread, free.

'Are you OK, Jojo?' Miss Larkin asks, and I notice that fat tears are falling on to the picture, making the colours blur. I scrunch it up, watching the black paint turn everything grey and dirty.

That night I dream of the stream as it used to be, the grass lush and green and the water sparkling silver. Sometimes it feels like everything beautiful gets spoiled in the end, and you can't fix it, no matter how much you want to.

The next day I tell Miss Larkin about the blackbird and the blue garden twine, and after break she walks us all down to the stream to pick up litter. She pulls the doll's pram from the hedge, scoops rusty cans out of the water with a little net.

'Was the water always this dirty?' Miss Larkin asks, while the rest of us pick blue twine and ring pulls and sweet wrappers off the grass. 'I think perhaps we should write to the council, see what's going on.'

The following day Miss Larkin says we'll be doing a project

on pollution and looking after the earth, and we watch a TV programme about plastic in the oceans. Lucy Bell hides behind her hands and vows never to use a plastic straw again. Kiran Kaur, the toughest boy in the class, starts to cry and has to borrow a handkerchief. We decide to ban plastic from the classroom and the school garden, to get our parents to recycle. We write to the council about the dirty water, and someone writes back to say that they're investigating a local factory, which has been tipping waste products into the stream. There's going to be a court case and a hefty fine and a clean-up operation, it seems.

Maybe sometimes things *can* be fixed.

The dream comes over and over, a glimpse of green and silver. I try again to paint it, and this time it works a lot better.

Miss Larkin asks if she can borrow it to show to the head teacher, because he's been talking about putting a mural on the end wall of the school hall and, after all, Silverbrook Primary is named after the stream.

The head teacher agrees that it would be the perfect design, and work starts the following week, with

Miss Larkin and some of the parents standing on tall ladders to map the outlines, and the whole of Year Six helping with the rest. We mix up a dozen different shades of green to paint the grass, and there's real silver paint to add sparkle to the water.

The local newspaper comes to take a photograph of the mural, and Miss Larkin tells the journalist it was my design.

'It was just a dream,' I explain. 'A dream of green and silver.'

Miss Larkin smiles. 'Sometimes,' she says, winking at me, 'if enough people share the same dream, and work hard to make it happen . . . it can come true.'

I think of the stream, cool and clean and peaceful again. I think of Lucy Bell, who just this morning held a cake sale to raise money for an ocean clean-up charity, and Kiran Kaur, who has been making placards and says he's going to the School Strike for Climate Change next week. I think of our school, which is on track to be the first primary school in Westleigh to get rid of single-use plastic. I think those things are pretty awesome.

And I think Miss Larkin is right.

Doris,
THE CHICKEN WHO SAVED THE WORLD

Written and illustrated by
MINI GREY

You'll never believe this, I know, but, once upon a time, people used to eat animals.

I know – unbelievable, isn't it?

Well, this is the story of how it all changed.

This is the story of one brave chicken clucking in the wilderness.

This is the story of Doris the Hen.

Our story starts with an unusual egg who grew up to be an unusual chick. The chick's name was Doris, and what made Doris so very unusual was that she liked to read. Doris loved fairy stories about pigs and wolves and happy farms where chickens pecked in green fields, pigs played in meadows and cows ambled across grassy hillsides. When she slept, Doris dreamed of happy farms.

But when she woke up she was always crammed in a chicken shed with a thousand other chickens, crowded and bored and worried.

Now a rat named Basildon lived near the chicken shed. It was Basildon who brought Doris new books each day, and in return Doris would read to him, which Basildon found very soothing.

And one day a thought came to Doris.

'Basildon,' she said. 'You go in and out of the Chicken Shed. Could I go in and out too?'

'Well, kid, of course you could,' replied Basildon. 'I will show you. We can leave today.'

And so it was that Doris and Basildon found themselves squinting in the daylight and sniffing the sweet outside air and hitching a ride towards town on a rubbish truck.

'These I recommend,' said Basildon as he and Doris jumped off near a Mesco's Superstore – 'rich pickings.'

Doris blinked in the brightness of the Mesco food aisles, amazed by the dazzling array of wonderful packages.

Cornflakes! Cat food! Ketchup!

But then Doris found the meat aisle.

Sausages. Drumsticks. Steaks. Mince. What is this stuff? Doris had never seen anything like it before.

But Doris is a chicken who can read. So she had a look at the ingredients on the packets.

And suddenly she knew the truth. The fields. The meadows. The pigs. The cows. The chicken sheds . . .

THEY EAT US.

They eat all of us.

But if they knew us, thought Doris, *they wouldn't*. She must explain.

So she went to the supermarket manager.

'All this meat was once an animal. You wouldn't eat us if you knew us!'

But all the supermarket manager heard was: 'BUK buk buk BUK BUK buk buk buk-buk BUK!'

'This chicken is causing a disturbance,' he said to the security guard. 'Take it away.'

So Doris was escorted out of the supermarket.

'And DON'T come back again!' added the security guard.

But Doris is an unusual hen. And Doris can read. Doris found the library. Doris found the Electronics for Chickens section. And Doris read.

Doris enlisted the help of Basildon the Rat, who knew well the treasures to be found in the town dump. On the dump, Doris and Basildon collected: a transformer, a microphone, spark plugs, diodes, a food mixer and a lot of wire.

They worked and built and tested.

They changed and adjusted and tested again.

And they built the world's first Universal Translaterizer.

Basildon tuned it in . . . bzzzzz . . . zzzzp . . .

'Buk BUK BUK B – TOLD YOU IT WOULD WORK, BASILDON!' said Doris.

'But how will we tell THE WHOLE WORLD?' asked Basildon.

Doris hatched a plan. She read and researched until she found the address of a billionaire investor. This billionaire investor had not had much luck in the past (he had invested in such dubious inventions as the rubber doughnut, the exploding wine bottle and the cheese magnet), but with Doris that was about to change.

'Where did you get that?' asked the billionaire investor breathlessly, when Doris showed him her invention.

'I MADE IT MYSELF!' replied Doris through the translaterizer.

'Is it —' gasped the investor. 'It can't be . . . a Universal Translizerator?'

'NO,' said Doris, 'IT'S A UNIVERSAL TRANSLATERIZER! I MADE IT MYSELF.'

'Chicken!' cried the billionaire investor.

'For the first time in my life I see a REALLY GOOD investment opportunity!'

So, the billionaire investor and Doris went into business . . .

. . . making Universal Translaterizers for every farm animal in the country.

Which changed everything.

Because you can't eat someone who can talk to you, can you?

That would be simply too rude.

And so eating meat really just stopped being something people did, after some difficult shopping choices.

From then on things became a bit different – and people realized they could give a bit more space to everybody who wasn't human.

And that's the story of how one chicken changed the world. Which just shows that anyone can make a difference, even if they are a chicken.

And that's why, on 11 August every year, we honour the chicken who made the Invisible Visible, who made Meat Talk, who changed Meals forever.

We have . . .

DORIS DAY!!!!

(Well, us chickens do.)

The Special Pumpkin

FROM

TALES FROM THE CARIBBEAN

WRITTEN BY TRISH COOKE

Illustrated by Margaux Carpentier

Maman was old and she knew it. Her hair was thinning and what was left of it was grey. Her body ached and she could hardly walk. Her husband had died many years before, and her sons, their wives and their children had moved away from Martinique to live in far-off countries.

Maman had no visitors, save her greedy neighbour, Madame Jalousie. Madame Jalousie would only pass by Maman's house to show off about how good her life was and to tell Maman how well her own children were doing and how often they visited her.

Madame Jalousie liked to brag about all sorts of things. Often she would brag to Maman about all the different

vegetables she had growing in her garden. She knew well that Maman's garden no longer bore fruit or vegetables. Watercress was the only thing that grew in Maman's garden these days.

Maman just listened to Madame Jalousie with an open heart and never asked for anything. Madame Jalousie never offered Maman anything either, even though she knew that all Maman had to eat was wild watercress.

So Maman ate watercress stew, watercress soup, watercress pie and watercress cake, and she dreamed of all the wonderful fruits and vegetables she used to eat when she was younger, when her garden was full. Maman would dream about eating a juicy mango and sucking the pulp right down to the seed, or eating sour sop or breadfruit, or even a hearty chicken stew with dumplings, or fried fish and johnnycakes. But Maman never grumbled. Instead she rejoiced. Maman had had a full and joyous life with her family and she had many fond memories. So when Madame Jalousie visited Maman empty-handed, Maman just smiled and wished her neighbour well.

One day Maman was sitting on her verandah when a tiny, beautiful bird landed at her feet. The bird's wings had some feathers the colour of the turquoise blue sea, and some feathers the colour of a warm orange sunset.

'What a beautiful bird!' she said to herself. 'And how lovely that you have chosen to spend a moment with me.'

But when the old lady looked closer at the bird, she noticed that one of the wings on the bird was broken. Feeling sorry for the bird, Maman picked it up carefully so as not to hurt its fragile body and tenderly put it against her chest to keep it safe and warm.

'There, there . . .' she said. 'Now don't you worry, I'll take care of you.' And that was what Maman did. Every day she gave the bird clean water to drink and shared with it her watercress. She kept the bird safe, away from harm, and she grew to love it with all her heart. She sang to it every day:

'Bel oiseau, bel oiseau,
Je vais vous faire forte,'

which means,

'Beautiful bird, beautiful bird,
I will make you strong.'

Slowly, slowly, the bird began to get stronger and stronger, and gradually the broken wing began to heal. Finally, one day, the bird's wing was well enough for it to fly again. Maman

watched the bird fly around her all day long and finally she decided that it was time to let the bird go. The old lady had enjoyed the company, but she knew that the best thing for the bird was to let it fly out into the sky. So one day she put the bird on the palm of her hand and said,

'Allez, petit oiseau,'

which means,

'Go, little bird.'

And the bird flew away, up into the sky, gently flapping its wings.

With the bird gone, Maman was once again alone, except from the occasional visits from her greedy neighbour, Madame Jalousie. Maman would often look up to the sky to see if her friend, the beautiful blue and orange bird, was passing, but it never came back. Maman didn't grumble. She was thankful that she had shared a lovely time with the bird and she enjoyed the memory.

Then, to Maman's surprise, one day as she was sitting watching the sun come up, she heard the gently flapping wings above her head. When she looked up, it was none other than the beautiful blue and orange bird that she had nursed. She was so glad that the bird had come back.

But the bird had not come to stay. Instead, it dropped something from its beak and flew away again. The old lady was sad to see it fly away so quickly, but she looked on the ground to see what it had left her and there, at her feet, lay a small pumpkin seed.

'Oh, a pumpkin seed!' said Maman. 'Thank you. I will plant the seed in my garden.'

Maman took the seed to the bottom of her garden and she planted the seed very carefully in the soil. Every day she watered her pumpkin seed and talked and sang to it:

'*Petite graine, petite graine,*
Je vais vous faire forte,'

which means,

'*Little seed, little seed,*
I will make you strong.'

And, as the sun shone on the seed, after a few days the

seed began to sprout. Maman was so excited when she saw the tiny shoot that she began to sing to it even more sweetly than before:

'Petite graine, petite graine,
Je vais vous faire forte.

Little seed, little seed,
I will make you strong.'

Before long the shoot grew into a vine that began to flower. Maman loved her pumpkin plant and she encouraged it to grow. And, soon enough, a pumpkin did begin to grow. Maman loved her pumpkin and sang even more sweetly than before.

While she waited for the pumpkin to ripen, Maman imagined all the dishes she would be able to make – pumpkin soup, fried pumpkin, roast pumpkin, grilled pumpkin, pumpkin stew, pumpkin pie . . . She couldn't wait to taste it.

At last the day finally arrived and the pumpkin was ripe. Maman's mouth watered as she brought it inside to carve it up.

But when Maman sliced the pumpkin, a strange thing happened.

Inside, instead of the pumpkin flesh and seeds she expected, it was filled with all of Maman's favourite dishes from the days when she used to eat with her family. There was a hearty chicken stew with dumplings, and fried fish and johnnycakes. There was breadfruit and sour sop and the flesh of the juiciest mango. Maman could not believe her eyes! She ate and ate and ate until her belly was so full it felt like it was about to burst. There was still plenty of food left in the pumpkin.

'So much food!' Maman said. 'Much too much for me alone, I will take some to my neighbour.' And that is what Maman did. She wrapped the rest of the special pumpkin in paper and brought it to Madame Jalousie.

'I have brought you some food from my very special pumpkin,' said Maman. Madame Jalousie tore open the paper. When she saw all the food inside, she ate greedily without so much as a thank you. But Maman wasn't expecting any thanks from Madame Jalousie, so it didn't make any difference to her. Maman was only glad that the food in the pumpkin wasn't going to go to waste.

Maman went home and, before she went to bed, she thought about how the little bird had been so kind to bring

her the pumpkin seed, and she was thankful for her blessings.

The next day, when Maman woke up and looked out into her garden, she found a wondrous surprise. There in the garden was another ripe pumpkin! Maman was so excited, and once again when she cut the pumpkin open she saw it was full of even more of her favourite food. There was saltfish, oxtail stew and souse. There was sweet potato and christophine and the sweetest passion fruit. Maman was so happy. Once again she had been provided with a feast of a meal. Maman ate and ate and ate until her belly was so full it felt like it was about to burst. Still there was plenty of food left in the pumpkin.

'I'll bring the rest for Madame Jalousie,' Maman said and, just as before, she wrapped the remainder in some paper and brought it to her neighbour. When Madame Jalousie saw Maman approaching, she ran out to her and snatched the food from her hands.

'The pumpkin you brought yesterday was so nice!' she said greedily, and ate up all the food without a word of thanks to Maman. Maman left Madame Jalousie stuffing the food in her mouth and smiled. She was just glad that the food was not going to be wasted.

The next day when Maman woke up there was yet another pumpkin in her garden, filled with more of her favourite

foods. After eating enough to fill her belly, Maman brought Madame Jalousie the rest. But this time, as Madame Jalousie ate greedily from the pumpkin, she stopped Maman from leaving and said, 'You must tell me how it is that you get to grow such special pumpkins!'

And Maman told her how the beautiful blue and orange bird had appeared in her garden with the broken wing. She told her how she had nursed the bird and how, when the wing was better, she had let the bird fly away. She told Madame Jalousie that the bird had come back and left her the pumpkin seed, and how she had planted the seed and cared for it, and how the pumpkin had grown ripe and she had cut it open to find all the food she loved.

'Then I will get a pumpkin, just like yours!' said Madame Jalousie.

The next day Madame Jalousie sat on her verandah, looking up at the sky to see if a blue and orange bird would fly to her too. The sky remained clear. When Maman came with the special pumpkin food to give her, as she had done before, Madame Jalousie said, 'Go away! I don't want your leftovers! I am going to have my own pumpkin!'

Every day Madame Jalousie looked in the sky for the blue and orange bird, but it was nowhere to be seen.

And then, finally, to Madame Jalousie's delight, one day a beautiful blue and orange bird landed on the fence of her verandah. As the bird was about to fly away again, Madame Jalousie grabbed it. Without a moment's thought she twisted the bird's wing until it snapped. The poor bird shrieked with pain. Then Madame Jalousie threw it into a dark corner of her room. She threw some scraps of food after it.

'Hurry up and get better!' she said. 'I want my pumpkin!'

With no love in her heart Madame Jalousie checked on the bird every day to see if the wing was better, but it would not heal.

'Hurry up and get better!' she said. 'I want my pumpkin!'

Madame Jalousie became tired of waiting and after three days she took the bird outside and said,

'Allez-vous en! Allez-vous en!'

which means,

'Go away! Go away!'

The poor bird tried to leave but it could hardly fly on its broken wing.

'Volez, oiseau!' Madame Jalousie said. 'Fly away, bird!' And she picked up the bird and threw it out. The bird tried with all its might to fly and eventually flapped the good wing so hard that it could fly away from the evil woman. As the bird flew away Madame Jalousie shouted after it, 'Hurry up! I want my pumpkin!'

Well, weeks and weeks went by and there was no sign of the bird with the pumpkin seed. Madame Jalousie grew more and more impatient.

'Where is that stupid bird!' she moaned. 'I want a pumpkin seed just like Maman's. I want a pumpkin with food in it, just like Maman's!'

But there was still no sign of the bird with the seed and Madame Jalousie grew more and more vexed.

'That stupid bird is never coming back!' she said angrily. 'I hope it is dead!'

And as she said that, the sky grew dark and thunder began to rumble in the sky. That night there was a terrible storm. The next day, when Madame Jalousie went out on to her verandah, she heard the sound of gently flapping wings above her head. Lo and behold, when she looked up she saw the blue and orange bird had returned.

'Looks like your wing has got better then!' Madame

Jalousie said, without any care. 'Now where's my pumpkin seed? Give it to me!'

The bird dropped something from its beak and flew away again. Madame Jalousie was glad to see the back of the bird and called and jeered as it flew away.

'About time! And good riddance!' she shouted, and then she bent down to pick up her pumpkin seed.

'Hooray! Now I can plant my seed and get my pumpkin!' she said ungratefully. She put the seed in her garden, paying no mind to where she planted it. She did not care for it at all. All she was bothered about was getting a pumpkin.

'Seed! Hurry up and grow!' she shouted. 'I want my pumpkin!'

Eventually the seed began to sprout. Madame Jalousie grew more restless.

'What's taking so long?' she shouted. 'Hurry up, I want my pumpkin now!'

After some time the shoot grew into a vine, which began to flower, but still Madame Jalousie grew more and more restless.

'I want my pumpkin!' she shouted. 'I want my pumpkin!' Slowly, slowly, the pumpkin grew, but Madame Jalousie knew

that she could not have it until it was ripe.

'Hurry up and ripen, you stupid pumpkin!' she shouted. 'You're taking too long!'

At last the day finally arrived when Madame Jalousie's pumpkin was ripe. Madame Jalousie took up a machete and she cut into the pumpkin.

But to her horror when she looked inside, instead of all the lovely food that Maman had found, Madame Jalousie's pumpkin was filled with spiders and cockroaches and mosquitos and scorpions!

'Euuuuuuugggghhhh!' cried Madame Jalousie. 'Where's my food? I want food in my pumpkin, like Maman!' But there was no food to be found, only creepy-crawlies.

Madame Jalousie was so disgusted at what she saw that she ran away from all the nasty creatures coming out of her pumpkin and she was never seen again.

As for Maman, she lived the rest of her days enjoying the delicious food from all of the special pumpkins that grew in her garden.

When I was 8, my big dream for the future was to be Dr Nikki the make-up artist. I wanted to be a doctor on weekdays so I could make people feel better physically, and a make-up artist on the weekend to help people feel more confident within themselves. I wanted to do this more than anything because I was quite unwell and doctors became my constant. They were so lovely to me and always put me at my ease, and so I dreamed of being able to do the same for others . . . I also wanted to do something with make-up in my spare time. Make-up was like magic to me – I found it so amazing how a little bit of make-up could transform someone's confidence and make them feel stronger; I loved how it could be an outlet to express your creativity.

NIKKI LILLY, YOUTUBER AND PRESENTER

I magine being able to see things no one has ever seen before, visiting a different time: my dream is to invent a time machine! If I had a time machine, if I could travel to any year I wanted, if I could see how many people used to ive in the past and will in the future, then the world could be a better place.

The more I think about it, the more I want to explode! My time machine would change the world; fixing things before they happen in the past which would change the world now. My time machine would let me travel to the future, discovering the most unusual, imaginative objects ever — when robots have taken over the world! This is my big dream.

DAISY, AGE 11,
ST OSWALD'S CE VA PRIMARY SCHOOL

Big dreamers
aren't afraid
to start
small.

Written and illustrated by
SOPHY HENN

When I was 8, my only big dream for the future was to follow the dry stream bed as far as I could, encountering frogs in the pools left below the bridges.

I'll always remember the first time I saw a puffin, with its comical appearance and bright bill. It seemed otherworldly, a doorway to a new world of sea, islands and seabirds. And now I'm Chief Executive of the RSPB (the Royal Society for the Protection of Birds)!

Sadly puffins have dropped in number since then – but you can help us save them. Join Project Puffin by sending us a photo of a puffin you have seen, or visit one of our stunning nature reserves and see a puffin for yourself. With your help, we can continue to give our magical puffins a home.

#Puffarazzi

BECCY SPEIGHT, CHIEF EXECUTIVE,
THE ROYAL SOCIETY FOR THE PROTECTION
OF BIRDS (RSPB), AND MASSIVE PUFFIN FAN

A Necklace of Raindrops

WRITTEN BY JOAN AIKEN

Illustrated by Jan Pieńkowski

A man called Mr Jones and his wife lived near the sea. One stormy night Mr Jones was in his garden when he saw the holly tree by his gate begin to toss and shake.

A voice cried, 'Help me! I'm stuck in the tree! Help me, or the storm will go on all night.'

Very surprised, Mr Jones walked down to the tree. In the middle of it was a tall man with a long grey cloak, and a long grey beard, and the brightest eyes you ever saw.

'Who are you?' Mr Jones said. 'What are you doing in my holly tree?'

'I got stuck in it, can't you see? Help me out, or the storm will go on all night. I am the North Wind, and it is my job to blow the storm away.'

So Mr Jones helped the North Wind out of the holly tree. The North Wind's hands were as cold as ice.

'Thank you,' said the North Wind. 'My cloak is torn, but never mind. You have helped me, so now I will do something for you.'

'I don't need anything,' Mr Jones said. 'My wife and I have a baby girl, just born, and we are as happy as any two people in the world.'

'In that case,' said the North Wind, 'I will be the baby's godfather. My birthday present to her will be this necklace of raindrops.'

From under his grey cloak he pulled out a fine, fine silver chain. On the chain were three bright, shining drops.

'You must put it round the baby's neck,' he said. 'The raindrops will not wet her, and they will not come off. Every year, on her birthday, I will bring her another drop. When she has four drops she will stay dry, even if she goes out in the hardest rainstorm. And when she has five drops no thunder or lightning can harm her. And when she has six drops she will not be blown away, even by the strongest wind. And when she has seven raindrops she will be able to swim the deepest river. And when she has eight raindrops she will be able to swim the widest sea. And when she has nine raindrops she will be able to make the rain stop raining if she claps her hands. And when she has ten raindrops she will be able to make it start raining if she blows her nose.'

'Stop, stop!' cried Mr Jones. 'That is quite enough for one little girl!'

'I was going to stop anyway,' said the North Wind. 'Mind, she must never take the chain off, or it might bring bad luck. I must be off, now, to blow away the storm. I shall be back on her next birthday, with the fourth raindrop.'

And he flew away up into the sky, pushing the clouds before him so that the moon and stars could shine out.

Mr Jones went into his house and put the chain with the three raindrops round the neck of the baby, who was called Laura.

A year soon went by, and when the North Wind came back to the little house by the sea, Laura was able to crawl about, and to play with her three bright, shining raindrops. But she never took the chain off.

When the North Wind had given Laura her fourth raindrop she could not get wet, even if she was out in the hardest rain. Her mother would put her out in the garden in her pram, and people passing on the road would say, 'Look at that poor little baby, left out in all this rain. She will catch cold!'

But little Laura was quite dry, and quite happy, playing with the raindrops and waving to her godfather the North Wind as he flew over.

Next year he brought her her fifth raindrop. And the year after that, the sixth. And the year after that, the seventh. Now Laura could not be harmed by the worst storm, and if she fell into a pond or river she floated like a feather. And when she had eight raindrops she was able to swim across the widest sea – but as she was happy at home she had never tried.

And when she had nine raindrops Laura found that she could make the rain stop, by clapping her hands. So there were many, many sunny days by the sea. But Laura did not always clap her hands when it rained, for she loved to see the silver drops come sliding out of the sky.

Now it was time for Laura to go to school. You can guess how the other children loved her! They would call, 'Laura, Laura, make it stop raining, please, so that we can go out to play.'

And Laura always made the rain stop for them.

But there was a girl called Meg who said to herself, 'It isn't fair. Why should Laura have that lovely necklace and be able to stop the rain? Why shouldn't I have it?'

So Meg went to the teacher and said, 'Laura is wearing a necklace.'

Then the teacher said to Laura, 'You must take your necklace off in school, dear. That is the rule.'

'But it will bring bad luck if I take it off,' said Laura.

'Of course it will not bring bad luck. I will put it in a box for you and keep it safe till after school.'

So the teacher put the necklace in a box.

But Meg saw where she put it. And when the children were out playing, and the teacher was having her dinner, Meg went quickly and took the necklace and put it in her pocket.

When the teacher found that the necklace was gone, she was very angry and sad.

'Who has taken Laura's necklace?' she asked.

But nobody answered.

Meg kept her hand tight in her pocket, holding the necklace.

And poor Laura cried all the way home. Her tears rolled down her cheeks like rain as she walked along by the sea.

'Oh,' she cried, 'what will happen when I tell my godfather that I have lost his present?'

A fish put his head out of the water and said, 'Don't cry,

Laura dear. You put me back in the sea when a wave threw me on the sand. I will help you find your necklace.'

And a bird flew down and called, 'Don't cry, Laura dear. You saved me when a storm blew me on to your roof and hurt my wing. I will help you find your necklace.'

And a mouse popped his head out of a hole and said, 'Don't cry, Laura dear. You saved me once when I fell in the river. I will help you find your necklace.'

So Laura dried her eyes. 'How will you help me?' she asked.

'I will look under the sea,' said the fish. 'And I will ask my brothers to help me.'

'I will fly about and look in the fields and woods and roads,' said the bird. 'And I will ask all my brothers to help me.'

'I will look in the houses,' said the mouse. 'And I will ask my brothers to look in every corner and closet of every room in the world.'

So they set to work.

While Laura was talking to her three friends, what was Meg doing?

She put on the necklace and walked out in a rainstorm. But the rain made her very wet! And when she clapped her hands to stop it raining, the rain took no notice. It rained harder than ever.

The necklace would only work for its true owner.

So Meg was angry. But she still wore the necklace, until her father saw her with it on.

'Where did you get that necklace?' he asked.

'I found it in the road,' Meg said. Which was not true!

'It is too good for a child,' her father said. And he took it away from her. Meg and her father did not know that a little mouse could see them from a hole in the wall.

The mouse ran to tell his friends that the necklace was in Meg's house. And ten more mice came back with him to drag it away. But when they got there, the necklace was gone. Meg's father had sold it, for a great deal of money, to a silversmith. Two days later, a little mouse saw it in the silversmith's shop, and ran to tell his friends. But before the mice could come to take it, the silversmith had sold it to a trader who was buying fine and rare presents for the birthday of the Princess of Arabia.

Then a bird saw the necklace and flew to tell Laura.

'The necklace is on a ship, which is sailing across the sea to Arabia.'

'We will follow the ship,' said the fishes. 'We will tell you which way it goes. Follow us!'

But Laura stood on the edge of the sea.

'How can I swim all that way without my necklace?' she cried.

'I will take you on my back,' said a dolphin. 'You have often thrown me good things to eat when I was hungry.'

So the dolphin took her on his back, and the fishes went on in front, and the birds flew above, and after many days they came to Arabia.

'Now where is the necklace?' called the fishes to the birds.

'The King of Arabia has it. He is going to give it to the Princess for her birthday tomorrow.'

'Tomorrow is my birthday too,' said Laura. 'Oh, what will my godfather say when he comes to give me my tenth raindrop and finds that I have not got the necklace?'

The birds led Laura into the King's garden. And she slept all night under a palm tree. The grass was all dry, and the flowers were all brown, because it was so hot, and had not rained for a year.

Next morning the Princess came into the garden to open her presents. She had many lovely things: a flower that could sing, and a cage full of birds with green and silver feathers; a book that she could read for ever because it had no last page, and a cat who could play cat's cradle; a silver dress of spiderwebs and a gold dress of goldfish scales; a clock with a real cuckoo to tell the time, and a boat made out of a great pink shell. And among all the other presents was Laura's necklace.

When Laura saw the necklace she ran out from under the palm tree and cried, 'Oh, please, that necklace is mine!'

The King of Arabia was angry. 'Who is this girl?' he said. 'Who let her into my garden? Take her away and drop her in the sea!'

But the Princess, who was small and pretty, said, 'Wait a minute, Papa,' and to Laura she said, 'How do you know it is your necklace?'

'Because my godfather gave it to me! When I am wearing it I can go out in the rain without getting wet, no storm can harm me, I can swim any river and any sea, and I can make the rain stop raining.'

'But can you make it start to rain?' said the King.

'Not yet,' said Laura. 'Not till my godfather gives me the tenth raindrop.'

'If you can make it rain you shall have the necklace,' said the King. 'For we badly need rain in this country.'

But Laura was sad because she could not make it rain till she had her tenth raindrop.

Just then North Wind came flying into the King's garden.

'There you are, god-daughter!' he said. 'I have been looking all over the world for you, to give you your birthday present. Where is your necklace?'

'The Princess has it,' said poor Laura.

Then the North Wind was angry. 'You should not have taken it off!' he said. And he dropped the raindrop on to the dry grass, where it was lost. Then he flew away. Laura started to cry.

'Don't cry,' said the kind little Princess. 'You shall have the necklace back, for I can see it is yours.' And she put the chain over Laura's head. As soon as she did so, one of Laura's tears ran down and hung on the necklace beside the nine raindrops, making ten. Laura started to smile, she dried her eyes and blew her nose. And, guess what! as soon as she blew her nose, the rain began falling! It rained and it rained, the trees all spread out their leaves, and the flowers stretched their petals, they were so happy to have a drink.

At last Laura clapped her hands to stop the rain.

The King of Arabia was very pleased. 'That is the finest necklace I have ever seen,' he said. 'Will you come and stay with us every year, so that we have enough rain?' And Laura said she would do this.

Then they sent her home in the Princess's boat, made out of a pink shell. And the birds flew overhead, and the fishes swam in front.

'I am happy to have my necklace back,' said Laura. 'But I am even happier to have so many friends.'

What happened to Meg? The mice told the North Wind that she had taken Laura's necklace. And he came and blew the roof off her house and let in the rain, so she was SOAKING WET!

Carnival

WRITTEN BY NATHAN BRYON

Illustrated by Selom Sunu

ELI

Today is the day I've been waiting for ALL YEAR! It's Notting Hill Carnivaaaaaaaaaaaal!

I've been practising my dance moves whenever I can.

My mum's from Jamaica, and she has told me and my twin brother Devon ALL about it.

Mum said 2.5 million people attend Notting Hill Carnival – that's way more people than in my whole school!

Mum said people who dress up at Carnival are part of mas, and that stands for masquerade. The different Carnival bands all wear different mas, and when they

dance through the streets it's called playing mas! Sounds fun!

Mum said Carnival originated in Trinidad and Tobago, and a Trinidadian activist called Claudia Jones helped organize the first one in London in 1959.

Devon is thirty seconds older than me.

He says that makes him thirty seconds smarter than me, thirty seconds cooler than me and thirty seconds stronger than me!

But I think I have a BIGGER afro than him. We are twins but also best friends!

This is our first Carnival, and we have made a costume that we can wear together: a HUGE dragon! It is gold and proper shiny!

But this morning Devon got out of bed on the wrong side – that's what Mum said.

He says he doesn't want to come to Carnival with me. He wants to go with his friend Tom.

'Devon, you promised,' I say.

'I thought *we* were best friends.'

Devon says, 'We are, but Tom says wearing costumes is for babies and I'm NOT a baby.'

I don't need Devon to have fun.

Mum drops him off at Tom's house before she goes round to spend the day with Grandad (he says he's too old to go to Carnival these days!).

Dad takes me to CARNIVAL!

The music is LOUD, and it is coming from every direction. There are speakers everywhere, even on trucks!

The sun is blazing so I put on my super-cool sunglasses.

The food smells great. I can't see the food stalls as there are so many people in the way, so my dad says, 'Just follow your nose . . .' We are sniffing . . . all the way to the most delicious stall. Dad buys us jerk chicken with rice and peas, my favourite! YUM!

We are following the floats and lots of people are in mas. I think they look amazing! Everyone is smiling!

I try to put on the dragon costume, but it doesn't work with just one person, it just drags along the ground. Loads of people stand on it.

Dad tries to put on Devon's part of the costume, but he's just too big. I take it off.

Maybe wearing costumes *is* for babies. Maybe Tom's right.

DEVON

WOWWWWWWW! Carnival is a rainbow of colour!

People are partying on their balconies, waving at everyone passing by. Tom and I give a BIG wave back!

I do miss Eli, but I'm sure he's having fun with Dad. Plus I haven't seen Tom all summer holiday.

Lots of people are waving different flags. Mum gave me and Eli a Jamaican flag each. I grab one corner of mine and Tom grabs another, and we start waving it around.

We pass a man doing face painting, and he offers to paint my face for FREE because we have the same flag. Eli and I love getting our faces painted, but before I can say YES PLEASE, Tom pulls my arm. 'That's for babies.'

'The music is too loud,' Tom says.

I think the music is great. Every street corner is playing a different song.

Our bellies are rumbling, and our noses are guiding us towards the food stalls. YUM!

BUT Tom's mum has forgotten her wallet so we can't get any jerk chicken with rice and peas.

We see loads of people dressed in mas and they look like superheroes. Tom says only babies dress up, but that can't be

true because they are all adults!

I'm starting to wish I'd come with Eli. Eli always has fun wherever he is.

Suddenly Tom says he wants to go home – he doesn't like Carnival! I want to stay, but I can't.

I want to watch the floats with the steel-pan bands, but I can't!

I want to dance in the sun, but I can't.

We turn a corner and I see a group of policemen trying to dance ... but they look funny. When they move apart ... I see ... Eli getting his face painted as a dragon! He doesn't look babyish at all!

ROTI

I run over and give Eli a big hug! 'BRO, you look SO COOL!'
I say. 'I'm sorry for not coming to Carnival with you, bro. I
have the most fun when I'm with YOU!'

We say bye to Tom and his mum. Dad pulls out our dragon
costume . . . 'I want to be a dragon with you,' I tell Eli.

Eli may be thirty seconds younger than me, but sometimes
he is thirty seconds cooler than me without even trying.

We put on the dragon costume. And we start dancing in
the sun. People are taking photos of us. We look so GOOD!

We follow the steel-pan floats as the sun starts to set. We
dance with everyone, and it feels like one big family!

Mum was right: Carnival really is the best day EVER!

A MOST IMPORTANT
Lesson
FROM
TALES FROM INDIA
WRITTEN BY BALI RAI
Illustrated by Poonam Mistry

Akbar was just a boy of thirteen when he became emperor. Surrounded by luxury and revered by his people, he was occasionally guilty of arrogance. For his best friend and chief advisor Rajah Birbal, these rare lapses offered a chance to remind Akbar that, despite his great empire and all of his wealth, he was just a person like any other. So when one morning, after one of their long walks, Akbar attempted to better his advisor with a childish trick, Birbal decided to teach his friend a valuable lesson about life.

It began when Akbar challenged Birbal, as they sat drinking

fresh, cool water in the palace gardens.

'Tell me, Birbal,' said Akbar, 'do you know how many bangles your wife wears?'

Birbal shrugged. 'I cannot say that I've given it much thought,' he replied. 'Bangles are bangles, after all.'

'Ha!' Akbar exclaimed with pride verging on arrogance. 'So, you see her hands every day yet you do not notice how many bangles she wears. How can that be?'

Birbal, feeling annoyed, took a deep breath. 'Your Majesty,' he replied softly. 'Let us take a walk by the lake and I will explain.'

They finished their drinks and walked through the gardens and on to the path that surrounded the lake. The water shimmered in the sunshine and everywhere birds chorused in the trees and shrubs. At the far end, a small stone staircase led up to the emperor's private residence.

'You take these stairs every day, Your Majesty,' said Birbal. 'Tell me, how many steps are there?'

The emperor shook his head. 'I see what you are saying,' he said, 'but it is not the same thing. We do not notice things

as much as we notice the people around us. Your wife is a person, not a staircase, and you should know how many bangles she wears. Besides, I own everything, so I don't care if there are six steps on this staircase or twenty. Nor do I care if there are two roses on a certain bush, or many more. They are all mine, regardless.'

Birbal shrugged. 'Very well, Your Majesty. I must attend to my duties. May I be excused?'

Akbar grinned. 'What?' he asked. 'No response or new lesson? Perhaps I am becoming as clever as you, dear friend?'

'Perhaps,' said Birbal, before walking away.

The following evening, Akbar was strolling past the lake to his quarters, when he spotted a vagrant lying in his rose bushes. Disbelieving, he edged closer and saw that the man was a sadhu – a holy man – dressed in ragged clothing and a once-saffron turban now dulled with grime.

'You!' he barked. 'How dare you lounge so carelessly in my gardens! GUARDS!'

The sadhu raised his head but did not reply.

'You!' Akbar said again, wondering where his guards had gone. 'Get out of here this instant!'

Sleepily, the old man shrugged, stroking his ragged beard. 'Is this your garden, then?' he asked.

'Of course!' Akbar replied. 'This garden, the palaces that surround it, the lake, the trees, this entire kingdom belong to me!'

'And what of the mighty river to the east, or the jungles to the south?' the sadhu asked. 'Are they yours too?'

'YES!' cried Akbar. 'Do you know who I am?'

The sadhu shook his head. 'I know not,' he replied. 'And I care not . . .'

'But . . .'

'Ssh!' the old man ordered. 'Tell me this, oh splendid and wealthy man – to whom did these things belong before you?'

Akbar raised an eyebrow, and in that instant, his anger subsided and his curiosity grew. Who was this strange holy man with his questions? Akbar wondered if the man was a friend of Birbal's. It would be just like his friend to test the emperor so. Regardless, Akbar was a thoughtful person, prone to philosophical debate and open to the thoughts and words

of others. Perhaps he could reason with this man, and show Birbal that his was a truly inquisitive mind.

'Did Birbal send you?' he asked.

'I know not this Birbal,' the sadhu said. 'And I care not. Answer my question. Who owned these things before you?'

'Why,' said Akbar, 'my father, of course. You must have heard of the mighty Emperor Humayun?'

'No,' the sadhu replied. 'I have not. But tell me, then, who was here before your father?'

Akbar shook his head.

'That would be Emperor Babar – my grandfather . . .' he replied.

'And before him . . .?'

'I . . . I . . .' began Akbar.

'Think a moment,' said the sadhu. 'This garden, these roses, the lake, the palaces – these things are only yours during your lifetime – correct?'

'Well, yes, but . . .'

'And when you are gone, they will belong to your son, and his son after him, and so on . . .?'

'Yes, that's true, but . . .'

'Each person only owns these things for as long as they live on this earth, then?'

'Yes.'

The sadhu smiled, showing blackened teeth. 'We are but travellers in this world,' he told Akbar. 'We travel the road, and when we need shelter from the sun, we rest in the shade of a tree. But eventually we move on, friend. The tree, however, stays where it is, and shades the next traveller, and the next . . .'

Akbar found himself nodding. He had never considered such things, in such a way, before. He looked around at his beautiful, lush gardens, and at the magnificent building surrounding them. The old man was correct – Akbar was merely their latest owner, and he would not be the last.

'Oh, wise one,' he said. 'I hear your words and I agree with them.'

'Heed them carefully, then,' the sadhu replied. 'For each of us must die one day, and none will take these things with us. The world is not yours, or mine, friend. It belongs to us all . . .'

Akbar thought of his wealth, and the splendour in which he had spent his life, and he felt ashamed. His riches no more belonged to him than the water in a well, or the birds in the trees. To learn such a lesson, at the hands of this old man . . .

The sadhu stood wearily. 'But,' he said, 'if you insist I go, then I shall leave at once . . .'

'No, no!' said Akbar. 'Stay as long as you wish, and let us talk some more about the world.'

The sadhu smiled, and began to remove his turban. Then, spitting tree bark from his mouth, pulling away his fake beard and wiping his face clean, he turned to Akbar.

'Perhaps it would be better to continue indoors, Your Majesty.'

'Birbal – it's you!' Akbar exclaimed, and once again, he gave thanks that he had been blessed with such a wise and true ally.

'Now, Your Majesty,' said Birbal, 'about my wife's bangles . . .'

Akbar grinned sheepishly, shrugged and led his friend away.

The Thing

FROM

STIG OF THE DUMP

WRITTEN BY CLIVE KING

Illustrated by Edward Ardizzone

Something, or Somebody, had a lot of shaggy black hair and two bright black eyes that were looking very hard at Barney.

'Hallo!' said Barney.

Something said nothing.

'I fell down the cliff,' said Barney.

Somebody grunted.

'My name's Barney.'

Somebody-Something made a noise that sounded like 'Stig'.

'D'you think you could help me undo my feet, Mr Stig?' asked Barney politely. 'I've got a pocket-knife,' he added,

remembering that he had in his pocket a knife he'd found among the wood-shavings on the floor of Grandfather's workshop. It was quite a good knife except that one blade had come off and the other one was broken in half and rather blunt.

Good thing I put it in my pocket, he thought. He wriggled so he could reach the knife, and managed to open the rusty half-blade. He tried to reach the creepers round his legs, but found it was difficult to cut creepers with a blunt knife when your feet are tied above your head.

The Thing sitting in the corner seemed to be interested. It got up and moved towards Barney into the light. Barney was glad to see it was Somebody after all. Funny way to dress though, he thought, rabbit-skins round the middle and no shoes or socks.

'Oh puff!' said Barney, 'I can't reach my feet. You do it, Stig!'

He handed the knife to Stig.

Stig turned it over and felt it with his strong hairy hands, and tested the edge with a thumb. Then instead of trying to cut the creepers he squatted down on the ground and picked up a broken stone.

He's going to sharpen the knife, thought Barney.

But no, it seemed more as if he was sharpening the stone. Using the hard knife to chip with, Stig was carefully flaking tiny splinters off the edge of the flint, until he had a thin sharp blade. Then he sprang up, and with two or three slashes cut through the creeper that tied Barney's feet.

Barney sat up. 'Golly!' he said. 'You are clever! I bet my Grandad couldn't do that, and he's very good at making things.'

Stig grinned. Then he went to the back of the cave and hid the broken knife under a pile of rubbish.

'My knife!' protested Barney. But Stig took no notice.

Barney got up and went into the dark part of the cave.

He'd never seen anything like the collection of bits and pieces, odds and ends, bric-à-brac and old brock, that this Stig creature had lying about his den. There were stones and

bones, fossils and bottles, skins and tins, stacks of sticks and hanks of string. There were motor-car tyres and hats from old scarecrows, nuts and bolts and bobbles from brass bedsteads. There was a coal scuttle full of dead electric light bulbs and a basin with rusty screws and nails in it. There was a pile of bracken and newspapers that looked as if it were used for a bed. The place looked as if it had never been given a tidy-up.

'I wish I lived here,' said Barney.

Bear at the Paw House

WRITTEN BY MEGAN RIX

Illustrated by Sally Anderson

The giant black Newfoundland dog lay fast asleep on top of the hill overlooking Loch Marron, in Scotland. Watching over him was a small rust-coloured piglet. The dog's legs twitched as he dreamed he was once again swimming against crashing waves. He whimpered and the piglet made soft comforting grunts. The dog's eyes flickered and he gave a shuddering cry of despair as he remembered his family being swept away from him. The piglet's snout nudged at the dog's soft fur. The dog's dark-brown eyes opened. He blinked in the sunlight, gave a whine, and sniffed at the salty scent of the distant sea.

'Bear!' a voice shouted from the bottom of the hill. 'Breakfast time!'

The dog looked at the piglet, gave a wag of his tail and raced down the grassy hill with the piglet right behind him. At the bottom Bear lolloped past the paddock and the duck pond and the stables. The piglet ran after the dog with shorter but faster-moving legs as they headed past the orchard where the rescued chickens were pecking at their breakfast corn.

'Rusty – food!' the same voice called.

The piglet squealed and overtook the dog as they ran by the barn where the sheep, cows and goats lived, to the courtyard where Helen, who ran the Paw House Animal Sanctuary, was waiting for them.

'Where have you two been?' she asked, as she put two

brimming bowls of food on the ground. Bear and Rusty were too busy eating to answer her.

Helen smiled as she watched the big dog wolfing down his breakfast. When he'd first been brought here, late one stormy night a few months ago, he'd been dangerously thin, his fur matted and one of his paws infected. His rescuers hadn't known how long he'd been stranded on the small uninhabited island off the coast of Skye before the fishing boat spotted him and picked him up.

'Must have been living on gulls' eggs and fish,' the rescuers told her.

Bear looked a lot different now. His paw was completely healed, his coat shone and no one would call him skinny.

The big dog looked up at Helen and then back at his empty bowl with a meaningful look.

'It's all gone!' Helen laughed. 'At least for now.'

Some prospective adopters were coming to see Bear later. They'd probably bring something nice for him to eat with them.

But when the dog-loving people arrived later that morning Bear was nowhere to be found. Instead they were greeted by a very friendly brindled staffie-cross called Luna who'd been waiting for a forever home for a long time. Waggy-tailed Luna was almost dancing with happiness as she left with them.

Helen found Bear and Rusty in the pond with the ducks and ducklings.

'You two!' she said, pulling out her phone to take their picture.

At that moment one of the yellow ducklings stood up on Bear's nose and gave a surprised chirp as if to say *Where did all the water go?*

Helen was laughing so much she thought the photo might come out blurred – but it didn't. It was perfect.

'This is going on social media!'

Bear sank his head beneath the water and the duckling paddled back to his brothers and sisters.

The photo had been on the internet for less than an hour when there was a phone call.

'We think he might be our dog Brodie –'

'We were out kayaking off the Isle of Skye –' another voice interrupted.

'A seal made me jump –'

'I fell in the sea –'

'Brodie jumped in after him –'

Helen imagined the scene as the excited voices told her what had happened. Sea currents could be very strong around here. A dog, even a good swimmer like Bear, a Newfoundland with webbed feet, could be swept away. Fighting against the waves, dragging himself to the safety of the tiny island's shore. The gulls screeching at the intruder.

'May we come and see if it's him?'

'Yes, of course.'

'But what about his microchip?'

'It wasn't readable.'

Bear and Rusty were sitting on top of the hill when the car arrived the next morning. One of the dog's ears lifted as he heard the sound of excited voices, then his head tilted to one side; the voices were familiar. His dream, his family, his lost family . . . The next moment he gave a bark of recognition and joy as he

bounded down the hill with a bewildered Rusty squealing and
running after him.

'Brodie!'

Rusty stood next to Helen as Brodie poked his great furry
head out of the car window. It was time to go home.

'Come back and visit,' Helen called after them, as she lifted
Rusty up and cuddled him to her. 'Be happy, Bear.'

A GREAT
Adventure

Written and illustrated by
AL RODIN

Toulouse and Lautrec stole a Little Red Boat and set off to sea in search of a GREAT ADVENTURE.

The little boat wandered across the vast rolling oceans, while Toulouse and Lautrec kept watch for sea monsters and dreamed about finding a secret paradise island.

But they didn't meet any sea monsters, and they didn't bump into any paradise islands. Instead, the Little Red Boat drifted and drifted until the sky filled with thick moody Clouds and the Waves began to snarl and Toulouse suddenly realized that he hadn't the faintest idea where they were.

'Are we lost?' said Toulouse.

'No, we are not lost,' said Lautrec.

'Which way then?' said Toulouse.

'I will ask for directions,' said Lautrec.

But, as far as Toulouse could see, there was no one to ask. Between the deep, deep down and the infinity of up, Toulouse and Lautrec and their Little Red Boat were as significant as driftwood.

But Lautrec, who had never felt small, was not about to start now. She leaned over the side of the boat and spoke to the Waves: 'Do you know which way is home?' she said.

Salty spit splashed up, and dribbled down her nose.

Lautrec wiped her face with her sleeve and called out to the

Clouds: 'How about you up there? Can you help us get home?'

There was no answer. Toulouse and Lautrec listened to water slap against the boat as the Waves crashed all around. And then came the rain. It rained and it rained and it rained.

Toulouse hid under his hat. But, Lautrec tried again: 'We need your help. Please stop storming about!'

This time the Waves answered:

'We are NOT storming about!' they said. 'We are fighting with the Clouds. We want to be UP.'

At this the Clouds cracked a lightning 'HA!'

'UP is for US. We like the view and we will not share it. You snakes must stay DOWN.'

'WE WILL NOT STAY DOWN,' the Waves fumed.

'Oh, we are doomed!' said Toulouse.

'We are not doomed,' said Lautrec.

But the Clouds thundered and flashed. The Waves whipped and lashed.

And Toulouse and Lautrec and the Little Red Boat were caught in between.

'Excuse me,' shouted Lautrec, 'please stop your fight. We really do need your help to get home.'

The little boat was pummelled and tossed and tipped and flung —

'STOP!' shouted Lautrec, 'STOP STOP STOP!'

Toulouse tried pulling Lautrec back, but she kept going at the giants, all drenched and wild: 'Stop crashing, and spitting, and frothing, and splashing! Stop beating UP and booming DOWN, or me and Toulouse and our poor little boat, we will all drown!'

The Clouds paid no attention. The Waves didn't even pause to listen.

'Besides,' said Toulouse, 'YOU'RE THE SAME!'

'WHAT?' said the Waves.

'Excuse me?' said the Clouds.

'We are not the same,' said the Waves and the Clouds together.

'They are wet and splashy,' said the Clouds.

'They are floaty and foggy,' said the Waves.

'YOU ARE THE SAME,' said Toulouse. 'You used to be a Cloud!' he said, pointing at a Wave.

'And you used to be a Wave!' Lautrec said to a Cloud.

'You are both up and you are both down so there is really nothing to fight about!' said Toulouse.

Then everything paused – just for a moment – enough time for a shrug – before the Clouds plunged down and the Waves lurched up, and with a belch and a whack Toulouse and Lautrec and the Little Red Boat were shot out of the sea, to fizz through the sky.

'We are doomed!' cried Toulouse.

'We are not doomed,' said Lautrec.

'But we are lost! And we are flying through the sky! And my shoe just fell off!'

'I will ask for directions,' said Lautrec.

But before Lautrec could ask anyone anything, they were falling back down, down, down, to land in the sea with a PLOP and a SPLASH.

The Waves and the Clouds, however, had stopped fighting. It was calm. A tired sort of calm. The clouds were yawning, the waves were snoring and Toulouse and Lautrec clambered back on to the Little Red Boat.

'I'm afraid we might still be doomed,' said Lautrec with a shiver.

'We are not at all doomed,' said Toulouse. 'Look –'

On the horizon they could see the cliffs, and on top of the cliffs perched their grandmother's house. So between snoozing giants in a land of ripples, the Little Red Boat bobbed home.

'That was a great adventure,' whispered Toulouse.

Lautrec was already fast asleep.

My big dream is to become a teacher in a primary school, to help all the children reach their dreams and learn about the world because children these days don't always believe in reaching their dreams.

Now time has moved on: I am standing here teaching a class about the world. Suddenly, I see a girl looking teary. Her name is Millie. Millie has had some tough challenges in life but there was one thing she was really upset about: she didn't believe in herself. Every day we encouraged her that she could achieve her dream to be a doctor.

Years have passed. Millie is now older and . . . has achieved her dream to be a doctor! She now believes in herself with everything she does. She is so much more confident than she was when she was younger.

SOPHIE, AGE 11,
CASTLECOMBE PRIMARY SCHOOL

THE *Invisible* TRUTH

WRITTEN BY AMY SPARKES

Illustrated by Lesley Barnes

Charlotte pulled the book from the bookcase: *The Invisible Truth* by William Anderson. Her father's book was a passionate argument that a magical world somehow existed alongside their own. A world largely hidden, except in rare moments, where strange incidents reminded people of its existence. But such events were explained away, and the book was considered the ranting of a madman.

This hadn't stopped William Anderson. Since Charlotte's mother disappeared four years ago, he'd thrown himself into his work – devoting himself to discovering this otherworld. Charlotte hardly saw him now. Every bedtime he used to read her a story about the magic existing right under their noses. He would finish with the same words: 'Once you have been touched by magic, you are never the same again.'

But now, Charlotte saw sadness in his eyes, as he whirled away, searching for secret creatures. She longed to be alongside him, to see them with her own eyes –

'Charlotte,' said her father's voice.

Instinctively, Charlotte hid the book behind her back as she twisted round towards the doorway. Her governess stood beside him.

'Miss Rendell is waiting,' said her father. 'Do finish your embroidery today.' He smiled briefly, then left.

'Embroidery!' Charlotte groaned. She looked at the world outside the window and watched her father stride over a heather-covered hill towards a pine forest.

'You are a young lady,' Miss Rendell snapped. 'Try to act like one. At least your father knows your place.'

'He knows nothing!'

'Embroidery.' Miss Rendell narrowed her eyes and marched out of the room.

Charlotte sighed and replaced the book on the shelf. Why couldn't he understand the real Charlotte – the one which longed to explore the wild Scottish lands? Her eyes fell on a framed piece of embroidery on the wall.

'I'm not a fragile ornament to imprison behind glass,' she murmured.

'Charlotte!' barked Miss Rendell's distant voice.

No.

Not today. Never again! As if something inside her had snapped, Charlotte ran to the open lead-latticed window and half climbed, half tumbled out, landing on tufty grass below. She scooped up her petticoats and ran – somewhere, anywhere, away from embroidery. Adventure called.

Charlotte's throat ached as she flopped against a pine trunk. She sighed. Miss Rendell would enjoy reporting her absence –

A loud flapping noise came from inside the forest. Charlotte looked up. A flash of orange and crimson feathers. What was that? A golden eagle? No, too big. And the wrong colour. She crept forward, soft pine needles springy under her feet. Somewhere, wings beat again.

For the first time in her life, Charlotte felt truly alive. Blood pumped through her. Her eyes absorbed every detail. Then she heard it: a strange, eerie birdsong, unlike anything she'd heard before. The forest blurred into insignificance. The song was calling her, strengthening her – speaking to the girl with a heart for adventure and truth. Tears  welled up as she listened. She couldn't return to the house and be who her father wanted her to be. She couldn't . . .

The song ended. The features of the forest sharpened again. She had to find that bird! There was a swooping flurry of crimson ahead. Charlotte's heart leaped.

'Wait!' she called and began to sprint. Her dress snagged on a branch, she stumbled over a root, yet on she ran, her eyes fixed on the bird, with desperation she'd never known before –

And that was why she failed to notice the drop. The ground disappeared beneath her. Searing pain shot through her ankle, and at unthinkable speed the world no longer made sense as she tumbled down and down. She heard a thud – or did she feel it? – and blackness came.

Charlotte opened her eyes. Her head throbbed. She touched her forehead and saw blood on her fingers. She tried to move, but dizziness overwhelmed her. She closed her eyes. Her ankle was probably broken. No one knew where to find her. She was alone.

A rush of cool air stirred beside her. Charlotte opened her eyes again and gasped. Beside her stood the bird, more like a swan than an eagle. Its long, golden tail trailed behind it. The creature tilted its crimson head on one side, staring at Charlotte with black, beady eyes. Charlotte stared back, breathing quickly, not daring to look away.

The creature opened its golden beak a fraction and moaned a gentle, soothing sound. It leaned over Charlotte and a single tear rolled down its feathered face and landed on the gash on her head. Charlotte held her breath. Immediately, a comforting warmth spread through her body, from the head down. The dizziness and pain melted away.

'You did *that*?' Charlotte touched her head. 'What – what *are* you?'

The bird cooed softly again, then stretched out its huge wings. Before Charlotte could move, the creature gently clasped her in its golden talons and, with strength beyond its size, took to the sky.

Charlotte's heart leaped as they soared above the trees, laughing in astonishment as the wild breeze swept through her hair. Moments later, the bird landed beside the open study window.

'Thank you,' said Charlotte. The bird dipped its head, then flew away. Charlotte watched the crimson dot disappear in the distance, then she scrambled back through the window.

Miss Rendell's fury about Charlotte's ruined dress and her disappearance was wasted. Charlotte's mind was no longer in the room. And never would be again. It was on the strange bird.

At bedtime, her father arrived, clutching a book. Charlotte's heart thumped. She would tell him the truth, even if he locked her up. She could not be the safe, glass-imprisoned

daughter he wanted. He nestled on the side of her bed.

'Father –'

But she stopped as he opened the book and showed her a picture. '*The Legend of the Phoenix*,' he read, then looked at Charlotte. 'I saw something amazing in the sky this morning, above the forest. Sometimes you can live with someone for years and not truly know them.'

Charlotte stared at him. The air seemed to vanish from the room.

'I've been so busy with my work, I've failed to realize the invisible truth, unfolding before my eyes.' He took Charlotte's hand and looked at her searchingly.

Charlotte smiled and a tear trickled down her cheek. 'You know what they say, Father. Once you've been touched by magic . . .'

'. . . You're never the same again,' whispered her father. 'Miss Rendell will be leaving in the morning. I believe it's high time I had an assistant.'

Somewhere over the mountains, a phoenix sang.

The Cheetah's Whisker
A HABESHA STORY
FROM
TALES FROM AFRICA
WRITTEN BY K. P. KOJO
Illustrated by Mouni Feddag

There once lived a girl called Abeba. She lived close to a stream called Fafen Shet, in a village that sat in beautiful savannah plains. Her home was in Ethiopia, a country full of hills and rivers and one of the first places in the world where people farmed grain.

Abeba was the happiest girl you could imagine. She spent her free time playing tegre with friends and rode her father's shoulders while shouting, 'donkey, donkey, donkey.' When she spotted her mother, Mariam, coming home from work in the fields, she would run and skip around her, asking questions all the way home. Her father, Taddese, taught her how to write a kind of poetry called qene, which she liked to share with her parents while they had dinner.

Every day was wonderful for Abeba, except that every now and then she yearned for a little brother or sister to play with. She sometimes wrote qene poems about how a hand cannot make a loud sound without another hand to clap against, to remind her parents that she was lonely.

They would laugh and say: 'Be patient, child, everything happens in its time, in its own way.'

Mariam couldn't tell Abeba that she was not strong enough to have another baby. However, Abeba soon knew, for after falling sick during a season of flooding, her mother died.

Abeba became very quiet and would no longer go out to play tegre with her friends in the village any more. When she started playing again, she only played with her father. Taddese became her best friend, her teacher, her cook, her qene reader and still, sometimes, her donkey – even though by the time she turned nine she became a little heavy for the donkey to carry.

Then one day, Taddese told Abeba that she would have a new mother, because he was marrying a new wife.

'I know you've been sad,' he said. 'I've also been sad and lonely. Gelila is a kind woman, and I'm sure you'll love her.'

Abeba made a face and said nothing.

'She has two children as well,' Taddese added. 'A six-year-old girl called Elene and an eight-year-old boy – Girma. You'll finally have playmates!'

But Abeba wasn't very happy when Gelila moved in. She had had her father to herself for more than two years, and she wasn't ready to share him. Besides, nobody could replace her mother.

Although Gelila cooked much better than her father, Abeba never ate much when she made meals and only ate properly when her father cooked. She complained that Gelila didn't make specially shaped injera for her as her mother had and put in too little salt when making doro-wat – her favourite chicken stew.

Abeba also hated her stepbrother, Girma, because he opened her notebooks and read her qene without asking and he now played tegre with all her friends in the village. She didn't like sharing a room with two other children anyway and she didn't like that Elene got to wear all the clothes that she could no longer wear because she had grown too big.

She began to wander in the hills around the

village alone, thinking about ways in which life could be better. Abeba started to miss her mother all over again, even more than she had before. She wrote and sang sad songs called tizita:

Yesterday I danced a dream
but my arms today
are broken
only memories hold me close

She dreamed of her mother, remembering what her soft, brown skin smelt and felt like. She remembered how Mariam used to burn frankincense at the weekends, singing while washing clothes as her father looked over his students' work. How wonderful it was when she ruffled Abeba's short curly hair!

Gelila tried very hard to make Abeba feel special. She asked her what she would like to eat on Saturdays when they were all home together, she brought her little gifts from the fields, she taught her songs that she had learned while growing up, she offered to teach her how to draw portraits. No matter what she did, Abeba remained quiet and didn't respond.

As soon as the holidays came, Abeba begged her

father to send her to her grandmother's. She wanted to be close to someone that reminded her of her mother, who could tell her stories about her mother's childhood – someone who would understand how sad and lonely she was.

At her grandmother's Abeba cried every day for two days. Her grandmother tried to comfort her by cooking her favourite dishes and taking her to visit cousins that she had not seen for a while, but Abeba would not cheer up. Eventually her grandmother called and asked her what was wrong.

'If you came here to be sad,' said her grandmother, 'then you had better go back home. When I see my grandchildren I want them to be happy.'

'Ayat, I'm sad and I'm lonely. My stepmother doesn't love me and now my father doesn't have time to play with me any more. He's always with Gelila's children.'

'Abeba, your father will always have time for you. And how do you know that your stepmother doesn't love you?'

'I am not her child. I can see it in the way she talks to them. She doesn't do anything special for me; she ignores me.'

'Do you want her to love you?' asked her grandmother. Abeba didn't know what to say, because she had never thought about it, but she wanted to feel special again so she nodded. Her grandmother looked at her for a long time, then pulled her close to hug her. 'I think I know what is needed. This has not been done since my own grandmother was a little girl, but I think it could work for you.'

Abeba sat up, curious. 'What is it?'

'Well,' said her grandmother, smiling with her eyes just like Mariam used to, 'I can make you a love potion to give to her.'

'A love potion – that's exactly what I need,' said Abeba. She stood up and clapped. 'Yes, please.'

'Not so fast,' said her grandmother. 'It's a very complicated potion to make, but I can do it. It's just that there is one ingredient that you would have to get for me.'

'Anything, Ayat, I'm ready.'

'OK. The thing that I need to finish off the potion is the whisker of a cheetah.'

Abeba's jaw dropped. There was no one in the world more scared of cheetahs than Abeba. 'A cheetah's whisker?'

'Yes,' smiled her grandmother. 'Do you think you can get one?'

'Of course,' nodded Abeba, not wanting to give up. 'I'll go out tomorrow and start searching.'

Abeba knew that the cheetahs of the savannah slept for hours every day in shaded areas of high grass. When Abeba had gone to the edge of her grandmother's village to fetch water, she had never travelled much further – except in the direction of her own village. In every other direction, the isolated clumps of thorn trees looked scary. However, she set off the next day on her quest, knowing that she would have to go beyond all the paths she had known before, leaving behind the comfort of knowing where she belonged.

There weren't many places to hide in the open savannah. The hollows of abandoned anthills provided shelter here and there and sometimes there were caves. However, other animals lived in most of the caves and it was dangerous to intrude.

But Abeba was determined to have the love potion, so she carried on. Past the dark red sands that marked the edge of the village, past the stubborn clumps of low elephant grass that seemed to survive regardless of the weather, beyond the patchwork scatterings of spear grass and into higher clusters of mixed beard grass and lovegrass.

The grass was as high as her waist and made a pleasing, swishing sound as she walked through it. After a while she heard the distant trickle of a stream, so she climbed a nearby tree to look for it. She couldn't see the water itself, but Abeba could tell from the richer green of the grass towards the east, where she had to shade her eyes from the early sun, that it was there.

As she prepared to get down from the tree she saw a movement in the grass close to the stream and waited. She held her breath, her heart beating faster and faster, until she saw the creature through the grass; its thick tail, its distinctive markings, its smooth gait. It was a cheetah, a lone cat. She watched it move away from the stream and stop under a cloud-shaped bush. It stretched backwards then lay down to sleep.

Abeba got down from her tree and walked towards the cheetah. When she was close enough to hear the low rumble of the cheetah's breathing, she found another tree and crept even closer to rest beneath it and watch the sleeping animal.

Although she was scared, she felt close to the cheetah because, like her, it was alone. She was fascinated by the contrast between its white belly and the rest of its coat, like a secret it carried.

Abeba watched the cheetah all day until it woke again. It sniffed the air as though it sensed her presence. Its whiskers twitched and it let out a low growl as it yawned, tossing its head before it ambled back towards the stream. Abeba returned to her grandmother's, determined to return the next day and get closer to the cheetah.

While helping her grandmother cook

the spicy beef key-wat stew that evening, she thought about the cheetah's black tear marks that ran all the way down to the sides of its mouth, making it look sad and funny at the same time. Abeba hummed a tizita, but with a smile on her face.

Yesterday I danced a dream
and if today my
arms are gone
can my feet find a new rhythm?

She saved a large piece of raw meat from the key-wat to take with her the next day.

Abeba was up and by the cheetah's bush just after sunrise. The light threw her shadow behind her as she crept back to the tree she had found the day before to watch the cheetah.

The cat surveyed the horizon, now and then pausing to sniff the air. Abeba was as still as an anthill and breathed slowly through her mouth into her hands. She felt sure that the cheetah sensed her presence and it seemed to pause before settling down to sleep. When she was certain that it was in a deep sleep, Abeba left her hiding place and tossed the meat from the night before close to the sleeping animal.

When the cheetah woke up, it caught scent of the meat

and slunk towards it. It sniffed the meat cautiously, then lifted it into its mouth in one swift movement. As it chewed it sniffed the air, as if sensing Abeba's presence again, then made a soft growling noise before returning to rest under its bush.

Abeba watched the cheetah as she did the day before. She realized that she now found the sounds that the cheetah made familiar. She could tell when a growl was contented, when one indicated hunger or thirst. She could guess from a tone of purring that the big cat was about to sleep. She waited until the cheetah went towards the stream to drink and crept away for the day.

She returned the next day with more raw meat. This time Abeba did not wait for the cheetah to fall asleep. She stood up and tossed the meat towards the beast then walked slowly to her hiding place. She watched as the cheetah gobbled the meat and observed, stunned, as it seemed to toss its head in her direction. She thought that perhaps that was its way of saying thank you. Yes, she said to herself, yes.

Abeba headed back to her grandmother's with a skip in her step. She zoomed past the high clusters of mixed beard grass and lovegrass, the patchwork scatterings of spear grass, the stubborn clumps of low elephant grass and the dark red sands that marked the beginning of the village, to help her grandmother chop up ingredients for key-wat.

With the onion cooking in the niter kibbeh oil and her grandmother grinding more spices to add, Abeba crushed garlic cloves and paused to ask about the love potion.

'Ayat, when you get the whisker, do you chop it or grind it, or do you just boil it for flavour like you do with bones for soup?'

Her grandmother brushed a handful of spices into the pan over the nicely browned onions and looked at Abeba, a twinkle in her eyes. 'Just get it first,' she said. 'Get it and I'll show you.'

'OK.' Abeba took a piece of meat and wrapped it in leaves for the next morning.

At the cheetah's resting bush, the next morning, Abeba did not retreat to her hiding place after she tossed food to the cheetah. She crouched close by and watched it eat. She remained in the same position as the beast stared at her. It purred and sniffed the air in her direction, as if making sure that it was a scent it recognized, then turned to look across the wide expanse of the savannah. After a while, the cheetah growled softly and rose to go towards the stream.

Abeba returned daily with meat, moving closer to the cheetah each time.

One morning, after a few weeks of her visits, she was surprised to find the cheetah gone when she arrived. She thought that it might have walked to the stream early, but after a couple of minutes she heard a growl behind her. Abeba realized that she was surprised but not scared. She tossed the meat she had brought to the usual spot and the cheetah slunk past her, brushing its thick tail against her arm as it went to eat.

Feeling bold after her encounter, Abeba went to the cloud-shaped tree a little earlier the next morning to spring her own surprise on the cheetah. She crept up behind the big cat and stroked it along the thick patterned fur on its side. The cheetah purred, raised a large front paw in the air for a second and growled.

Abeba placed the piece of meat she had brought in front of the cheetah. As it ate, she reached out and pulled a whisker from its face, tucking it into a little fabric pouch that her mother had made for her when she was younger. She stayed beside the cheetah as it stared across the horizon and stood up with it when it rose to head to the stream for a drink.

Abeba went in the opposite direction, a bit sad to be leaving her new friend, but broke into an excited run as she approached her grandmother's home.

'I have it! I have it!' she screamed as she burst into the kitchen. 'I have the cheetah's whisker. Now we can make the potion.'

Her grandmother laughed and gave Abeba a big hug.

'Come and sit down, my child,' she said, leading Abeba to her bedroom.

'Now, tell me, how did you manage to get a whisker from a cheetah without getting any bites or scratches?'

Abeba sighed. 'I took my time. I watched it and tried to understand its habits. I knew that it had to trust me and I needed to lose my fear of cheetahs, so I was patient. I took it something to eat every day and got closer each time. After a while, I could tell that it expected me and waited for me. When I felt like it trusted me completely, when I felt that I could call it my friend, I sat beside it while it ate and pulled out a whisker.'

'That must have been very difficult for a girl like you; you're intelligent, but very, very, impatient,' said her grandmother with a knowing smile.

'Well,' said Abeba, 'I knew the whisker was important to you, to help make the love potion. Can we make it now?'

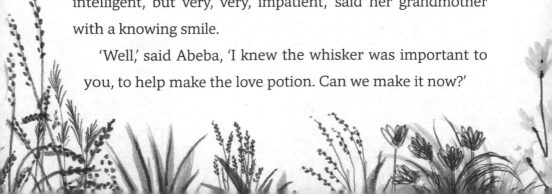

Abeba's grandmother looked her right in the eyes, holding the girl's face between her small, dark hands. 'Abeba, you don't need a potion. You were patient with a cheetah because you knew it was important to me. Now try being patient and attentive with Gelila and Elene and Girma because it's important to your father. You'll see it's a lot easier than making a love potion.'

Abeba nodded, tears welling in her eyes.

Her grandmother wiped her tears. 'And remember that I don't like to see you unhappy. It's important to me and your mother that you smile every day.'

The Tortoises Who
CAPTURED THE MOON

Written and illustrated by
ALEXIS SNELL

In a hot and dusty place beside a tall, beautiful, stripy building two tortoises lived all summer long. Above the tortoises, the building had a big round window which was brightly lit all day and all night. One tortoise was brave, the other . . . less so. Those were their names: Brave and Less So. They moved slowly, ate leaves slowly and chatted to each other ever so slowly.

'Oh, that looks like a nice leaf.'

'It really is, would you like one?'

'Yes please.'

A lot of their conversations went like this. The other animals who lived nearby thought they were slow and a bit boring. Brave and Less So didn't really mind, they were perfectly happy. Well almost.

One tortoise had a problem. The weather was getting cooler and the days shorter. It would soon be time to move up the hill and hibernate for the winter months, away from the stripy building with the round, bright window. It wasn't the building or hibernating or the hill that bothered Less So, it was the idea of moving away from the light that filled him with dread. He was afraid of the dark.

Less So was getting more nervous as the days grew chillier.

'Oh dear, what can we do?' Brave said. She really wanted to help her friend.

They stood together and looked up at the night sky.

'Wait, I have had an idea!' Brave was going to go on a voyage to capture the moon, so they had light every night.

'It might take me a few days . . .' she said.

Brave left the next morning. She climbed the hill all the way to the top.

'Hmm it's still too far away. Maybe it's down this hill and up the next one, maybe tomorrow night.'

On she went. Her stubby little legs were tired, but she was very determined. She simply *had* to help her friend.

The next day she walked all the way to the bottom of the hill and came to a small oasis surrounded by trees. A beautiful, tiny lake in the rocky landscape. The night came and to her surprise, as the moon came out above her, it also came out below her. The moon was reflected in the still water. She had never seen anything like it – not one moon but two! She wished Less So were here to see this. She spoke to a moth who was flitting about in the moonbeams.

'Hello there, Moth, perhaps you can help me? I'm trying to catch the moon,' Brave asked politely.

'Ha, there is no way you could get to the moon! I can fly and even I can't get that high. It's true then, tortoises' brains are as slow as their legs!' The moth flew off laughing.

Brave was so sad; the moth's words were hurtful and she had failed her friend.

She turned slowly, and headed home. It felt much longer on the way back and, worse than that, she had not brought the moon.

When she eventually got home, she told her story of the hills and the moon in the water and the moth. Less So was grateful for her efforts.

The rains came and it was too cold for the tortoises to stay any longer – they would just have to go. Away from the wonderful light from the window and up the hill they went. The rain was pouring down. They trudged through the mud and finally reached their winter home.

Just before they got into the dark little cave . . .

. . . Less So stopped.

For quite a while.

'Hang on . . . Oh, wait, I do! I have an idea!' And he did, in fact, have an idea.

As the sky grew dark, they dug a hole just outside their winter home, digging fast, the very one thing they could do quickly. It got darker and darker and they nervously waited to see if the plan had worked. Finally the rain ceased and the stars came out . . . and then the moon was in the sky and . . . hooray! The big round moon was reflected in the water below them – it shone into their cave and banished the dark – they had done it! It would be light all night long.

They settled down, happy, and slept for the whole winter.

Of course, with his eyes shut tight he could not see the light from the moon anyway, but sometimes knowing it's there is all that matters.

THE SPIRIT-WORLD OF
Childhood
FROM
BEATRIX POTTER'S JOURNAL
WRITTEN BY BEATRIX POTTER
Illustrated by Emily Sutton

I remember I used to half believe and wholly play with fairies when I was a child. What heaven can be more real than to retain the spirit-world of childhood, tempered and balanced by knowledge and common-sense.

I do not remember a time when I did not try to invent and make for myself a fairyland amongst the wild flowers, the animals, fungi, mosses, woods and streams . . .

If I have done anything – even a little – to help small children on the road to enjoy and appreciate honest simple pleasures . . . I have done a bit of good.

My big dream is to be a scientist and create a cure for epilepsy so poor people can live without having fits or seizures. I think that everybody deserves that life.

In this moment of time, my big sister, who has epilepsy, has changed my life. I had invented a lifesaving tablet! Me — who would have thought I could do that? My lovely sister, who is precious to me, just had to take one of these marvellous tablets from then on without any issues. Although there are tablets to reduce the risk of having fits, there is nothing like my tablets. They will help to remove the epilepsy but their memories will still be safe.

SO my dream came true and maybe many more can too!

LIBBY, AGE 11, CASTLECOMBE PRIMARY SCHOOL

My big dream is to be a famous dog walker and have a hotel for dogs for when their owners go on holiday and I look after them! It will be in England near a park so I can walk them. I will look after them and have assistants who will help me as well. I would like to have a really big swimming pool for the dogs to swim in and really cool hotel rooms with fancy beds for dogs, tea rooms and activity rooms!

My hotel would also have a big outdoor play area where dogs can play and a giant garden with bones and toy balls and a quiet play area where dogs can go and have some peace. There would be lots of food and water! In their hotel room there would be lots of chew toys and doggy biscuits for them when they are bored too. It would be amazing!!

KATIE, AGE 7,
ARDLEIGH ST MARY'S PRIMARY SCHOOL

DREAM
forever

Once upon a KNIGHT-TIME

WRITTEN BY HANA TOOKE
Illustrated by Ayesha L. Rubio

O nce upon a night-time, beneath the yellowy shimmer of glow-in-the-dark stars, two child-shaped lumps huddled beneath blankets. The only sounds were the gentle patter of rain on the window and the faraway hum of the streetlamps beyond.

Click.

A light, sudden and blinding, filled the room. There was a rustle of blankets from one bed, and a groan of annoyance from the other.

'What are you doing?' the boy child asked, shielding his eyes as he sat up.

He watched in bleary astonishment as his little sister clambered off her bed to stand on their octagonal bedside table.

'I be a knight of the octagonal table,' she said, raising her foam-finger sword up high above her head. 'Thou canst either fight me to thou death or join-eth me as a valiant protector of these lands.' She pointed her weapon down at the boy's throat. 'What's it to be?'

'You're not a knight,' the boy said crossly.

'I clearly am-eth,' the girl said, even more crossly, waving her free hand vaguely about her. 'Why would-eth I be wearing a suit of armour if I wasn't a knight?'

'You're wearing a nightgown. And that's a lampshade, not a helmet.'

'Thou hast clearly been hexed by an evil witch.' The girl lifted her lampshade helmet and smiled. 'Fear-eth not, for I can remove this evil curse.'

She spoke a few nonsensical words, then tapped him on the nose three times.

The boy glowered.

The girl's expression turned pleading. 'Please?'

The boy sighed. 'Fine.'

He shook his head, rubbed his eyes, and blinked a couple of times. When he looked again, he realized his little sister was absolutely correct. She was wearing a shiny suit of armour. It wasn't a lampshade on her head; it was a feather-plumed helmet. And it wasn't a foam finger she was wielding, but a gleaming longsword.

'All right then,' he said, getting to his feet. 'What should we do?'

'First, thou must speak-eth properly,' the girl said sternly. 'Thou canst not be a knight if thou doesn't speak-eth properly.'

The boy sighed. 'Uh. What-eth should-eth we . . . uh . . . do-eth?'

'I'm glad-eth you asked, O brave and noble fellow.' She handed him a giant pencil, which transformed into a battle-axe as soon as it touched his palm. 'Our mission is to save our queen over there.' She pointed to a large teddy on the other side of the room, which sported a wonky crown on its head.

The boy raised his battle-axe and took a step forward. 'Come on then –'

'No!' His sister grabbed his arm and nodded at the ground. 'Do you not see the danger that faces us?' She tapped him on the nose another three times. 'Look again.'

The boy blinked. The red shagpile rug was now a bubbling river of lava. The toy soldiers that lined the shelves on one wall all came to life, morphing into tiny, angry-looking trolls. And the blue curtains were now a rushing, frothing waterfall.

His sister was right.

This would be a difficult and dangerous journey.

'We should jump on to that boulder,' he said, nodding towards a former Lego box. 'Then on to that one.' He nodded to an ex pile of laundry. 'Then maybe we can reach her.'

'We must tread carefully,' the girl said gravely. 'Lest we wake-eth the ogre that slumbers deep below us, in the belly of the cold earth. It is she who wishes to eat the brains of our queen.'

'Lead-eth the way,' the boy said, perching his own lampshade helmet on the tip of his nose so he could see a little more clearly.

He watched his sister leap effortlessly on to the Lego-box boulder, then on to the laundry-pile boulder. She beckoned him to follow, so he swung his arms and jumped.

The helmet slipped off his nose and darkness surrounded him. His foot caught the edge of the Lego-box boulder and he crashed to the floor with a clatter and a thunk.

He lay there for a moment, heart beating wildly, ears straining. Footsteps, each as loud as a boom of thunder, reverberated across the ground.

'Oh no,' the girl whispered. 'You've awoken the ogre!'

The door opened with a slow creeeeeeeak.

A huge silhouette stood on the threshold.

The child knights blinked up at it.

'What is going on in here?' the ogre asked.

Her voice sounded soft and familiar, at first. But the boy

realized that must be a lingering effect of the witch's hex trying to trick him.

He tapped his nose three times.

'It's the middle of the night!' the ogre continued, this time in a more fittingly ogre-ish voice: deep and croaky, like a gargling walrus.

'Begone, foul beast!' The girl lifted her foam-finger sword.

The ogre crossed her arms and raised an eyebrow. 'Foul beast, am I?'

For a brief moment the ogre looked more like a smirking woman with kind, shining eyes. The boy tapped his nose again. This hex was strong!

'Thou will not-eth fool-eth us,' he said, raising his axe. 'We know thou art the evil ogre that wants to eat our queen's brains.'

'Oh no. I am the friendly ogre,' the ogre said, stepping into the room. 'All I want-eth is to ensure that the knights of the realm get-eth their sleep, for thou both hast school in the morning.'

The girl sheathed her sword and turned to the boy.

'Rest thine sword, my loyal champion. I can smell-eth the truth in her words. This be the virtuous ogre, not the evil one.'

The boy nodded solemnly. They let the ogre walk them back across the lava lake to their beds, then tuck them under their still-warm blankets.

The light clicked off.

'Good-eth night, my noble knights,' the good ogre said, before shutting the door and sealing them both in near darkness.

The glow-in-the-dark stars shone dimly above them.

As the ogre's footsteps retreated, the streetlamp hum rose again, sounding like a thousand fairy wings fluttering in the distance.

The rain patter slowed to a soothing waltz.

And the child-shaped lumps beneath the blankets began to snore softly.

My big dream is to see my nan in heaven. Time has gone by, and now I feel that the time has come to see Nana again. I miss her very much.

After a long day at school I came back home and went to sleep. This dream I had was like no other kind. I was transported to a magical place. There were walls like candyfloss and, amazingly, I saw my nan out of the window. I felt my heart melt. I wanted to run over to her and burst into tears.

But she was young. She had brown hair, blue eyes and was just the prettiest person. We started talking about her life in heaven and how it was really good. Before I knew it, I had woken up on my own, alone, in my bed. It was just a dream, the best dream.

TYLER, AGE 10, CASTLECOMBE PRIMARY SCHOOL

The Fairy Godmother

WRITTEN BY JACQUELINE WILSON
Illustrated by Nick Sharratt

My name is Hetty Feather and I'm six years old. Or I could be seven or even eight. I've lost count. We don't have birthdays at the Foundling Hospital. I feel as if I've been here a hundred years, but then I'd be an old, old lady, and I'm still a little girl. A very little one too, probably the smallest of all. But I'm one of the fiercest.

I long to go home almost every minute of the day, but this is my home now. We're called foundlings, all four hundred of us, in our scratchy brown uniforms and clompy boots. I wasn't 'found'. My poor mama handed me in to the hospital because she couldn't look after me. She wanted to keep me desperately, I know she did. She'll come and claim me back one day. I know that too.

It's not a hospital either, though lots of us get ill, especially in the winter because it's so cold and we have to have recreation outside even in the snow. When I lived in the country with my foster family, the best thing about winter was Christmas, but maybe we won't have Christmas here either.

I miss my foster family so much, especially my big brother, Jem. He is dearer to me than any blood brother. I write to him every week, but I never get a letter back any more. He promised me faithfully he would write regularly. I think Matron Peters keeps his letters out of spite.

I would like to tear Matron Peters in two and throw her away. I call her Matron Pigface because she has a face exactly like a pig, very big and pink and jowly, with little piggy eyes and fair lashes. I wouldn't be surprised if she started snorting one day. The matron for the senior girls is called Matron Bottomly and she looks even fiercer than Matron Pigface.

There are only two people I like here at the hospital. One is the maid, Ida. We all love Ida. She helps in the kitchen and she's a very good cook. Our breakfast and lunch and supper are so much nicer on Cook's day off, when Ida is in charge. She once made us a creamy rice pudding with a spoonful of red jam on top. She gave me two spoonfuls because I think I am her favourite!

The other lovely lady here at the hospital is Nurse Winterson. She takes us for darning every afternoon apart from Sundays, when we're stuck in the chapel practically all day. She is young and soft and sweet, and she smiles at us. She didn't tell me off for being clumsy when I started darning and stuck the needle in my fingers more than the holey sock. I soon learned.

It is very hard having to darn and darn and darn for hours at a time, especially now I have chilblains on my fingers. Nurse Winterson understands. She

reads to us to help the time pass. She is an excellent reader, almost as good as my brother Jem back home. She reads us all kinds of stories, and sometimes they are so absorbing I forget that I am Hetty Feather, with aching fingers, sitting on a stool in the grim Foundling Hospital. I am Robinson Crusoe on a hot desert island or I'm Jo March skating on a frozen pond or I'm Black Beauty galloping across a grassy field.

Nurse Winterson is reading from a volume of fairy stories at the moment, and they are truly magical. Yesterday she read us the story of Rapunzel, who was locked in a tower and her hair grew right down to her toes. I listened, spellbound. My own hair was chopped off when I was taken in to the Foundling Hospital. They do it to every girl who comes here. It was the worst thing ever, and I screamed and screamed. I loved my long bright hair, and my foster mother kept it clean as clean, washing

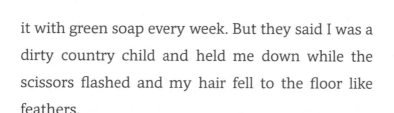

it with green soap every week. But they said I was a dirty country child and held me down while the scissors flashed and my hair fell to the floor like feathers.

At night I used to feel my sad stubble and cry. It has grown again now, so that I have a red cap of hair, but I so miss the feel of it tumbling about my shoulders. I pictured myself as Rapunzel, letting down my long hair from my tower room so that a handsome prince could climb up and help me escape.

Miss Winterson read us the story of Cinderella today, and it is even better than Rapunzel. I wept when poor Cinderella had to stay at home in the kitchen while her ugly sisters went to the grand ball, and how I wished I had a fairy godmother!

When we were changing into our nightgowns at bedtime, we all pretended to be Cinderella, swishing our skirts as if they were the finest silks and satins.

We stood on tiptoe, imagining our bare feet were encased in glass slippers.

'But only one of us will get to dance with the prince and it will be me,' I said, twirling round and round.

'As if a little squirt like you would ever dance with a prince, Hetty Feather!' said Sheila.

'I would so! And he will fall in love with me and want to marry me, I know he will!' I insisted.

I saw the prince in my mind. He was dressed in white and gold, a tall, strong, handsome man with Jem's dear face. He would rescue me from foundling drudgery and a future life as a servant. I would be a princess, and wear a different satin gown every day of the week, and a gold crown on my head, and my red hair would turn gold too and tumble down to my feet in silky waves.

I pulled the cover right over my head to blot out the girls' whispers, and pictured it with all my might,

and it seemed to be happening. I was at the ball, wearing a white dress that shone like the moon. I could feel its smooth rustling satin against my body, a joy after the stiff brown fabric of my foundling frock. I was wearing glass slippers that sparkled at every step, so light compared to the hard leather of my broken boots.

My ugly sisters were at the ball too, much older than me and grotesque in face paint and finery. One had the pink features and flattened snout of a pig, the other the sour, pinched expression of the dreaded Matron Bottomly. They simpered coyly as the prince advanced, but he strode right past them. He came up to me and swept me a splendid bow.

'May I have the honour of this dance, Miss Hetty?' he said, in the husky familiar voice I knew and loved.

'You certainly may, Prince Jem,' I said.

He took me in his arms and we whirled away to the music, my sisters Pigface and Bottomly gawping

in rage and envy. The prince and I danced all night long, and then he took me out on to the palace balcony.

'This has been the best evening of my life, dear Hetty,' he murmured.

'And mine, and mine!' I said.

He bent his head, and I knew he was going to kiss me, and my heart beat fast. I heard a chime in the distance, and thought it was the music striking up again. Then another chime echoed through the air, and then another.

Oh my Lord, it was the clock striking midnight! My fairy godmother warned me I had to leave the ball by twelve o'clock or my satin dress would turn back into my foundling frock and my glass slippers become broken boots.

I had to run faster than the wind! I broke away from the prince's embrace and rushed across the ballroom, elbowing my way through the crowd, dodging my ugly sisters, ignoring the footmen, running through the archway to the grand staircase. I scurried downwards, two steps at a time. One of my glass slippers fell off, but I didn't dare retrieve it. It was nearly midnight now – two more chimes to go. I gave a wild leap and landed badly, twisting my ankle.

The pain stopped me short and I went dizzy. I had to sit down on the stairs, clutching my ankle. I cried out. Then my eyes opened, but I couldn't see. The palace lights had gone out and there was blackness all around me. But I was still sitting on the staircase . . .

It was the grand staircase in the Foundling Hospital, and I was squatting there in my nightgown! I must have dreamed the Cinderella story, and walked in my sleep. I had to get back to my bed! If Matron Pigface caught me, she would lock me in a cupboard and throw away the key.

I heard footsteps. She was coming to get me! I struggled to my feet and then groaned, because my twisted ankle was real. The footsteps quickened. She was mounting the stairs! I covered my head to fend off the blows – but then felt a soft arm going round me.

'Shh now!' someone whispered.

It wasn't Matron Pigface. It was my dear friend Ida! She helped me up gently, supporting me under my armpit, holding something carefully with her other hand.

I couldn't help wincing as I tried to take a step.

'There now. Have you hurt your ankle? You poor little thing!' She put something down on the stair and then picked me up easily, as if I were a baby.

'I'm too big to be carried,' I whispered.

'Nonsense. You're light as a feather,' she said, and then chuckled softly. 'That's why you're called Hetty Feather!'

'How do you know I'm me? It's too dark to see,' I said.

'I'd know you anywhere, my love,' she replied, carrying me up the staircase, along a corridor, and then on up to her attic room in the servants' quarters.

She set me down gently on her hard little bed, wrapped her coverlet round my shoulders and lit a candle for me.

'Wait a minute, dearie,' she said, and then she whisked away.

I sat in the flickering candlelight, peering around her tiny room. It was very stark – one bed, one washstand, one jug, her servant's uniform hanging from a nail in the wall. But Ida had added little touches of her own: a rag rug was spread across the bare floorboards; a torn-out picture of a mother and daughter holding hands was tacked to the wall, opposite another colour plate of a little cottage with a cat on the doorstep and a dog in the garden.

Then Ida was back, holding a mug in her hand.

'I couldn't sleep so I crept downstairs to the kitchen to make myself a mug of tea. It's a wonder I didn't spill it when I sensed you sitting there on the stairs! It's still piping hot. Take a sip, Hetty, you're shivering,' she said.

'But it's your tea, Ida,' I protested.

'We'll share it – and we'll also share these.' Ida had a handful of sultanas wrapped in her clean handkerchief.

'Won't Cook see that some are missing from the sack?' I asked anxiously.

'Oh, she takes handfuls for herself all the time,' said Ida. 'We have a weekly order, because those greedy matrons are mad for their sultana puddings – with custard made from cream! It makes my blood boil to see them stuffing their faces when you poor little skinny mites have to make do with such meagre fare. You eat up, Hetty. And drink some more tea.'

We sipped and nibbled in turn, happily cuddled up on the bed together.

'This is lovely, Ida!' I said. 'I'm so glad I walked in my sleep now!'

'But you could have tumbled down all those stairs! You must tuck yourself into bed really tightly in future. Now let's have a look at this poor ankle,' she said.

'It feels much better already,' I told her.

'It's a little swollen.' She prodded it gently. 'I'll bind it up for you.'

She took her handkerchief and tied it tightly round my ankle.

'Is that better? Not too tight?' she asked anxiously.

'It makes a perfect bandage, Ida. Thank you very much,' I said. 'Why are you so kind to me?'

'Because you're a very special girl, Hetty Feather, and don't you forget it,' she said. 'You'd better hop back to your own bed soon, before the nurse on

night duty does her rounds.'

I tried standing up, testing my sore ankle. It hurt still, but not as sharply.

'Can I maybe come back another time, Ida?' I asked.

'If you're very careful not to get caught,' she said.

'I'd love to see your pictures properly in daylight,' I said. 'They look very pretty.'

'I dream that one day I'll be with my own daughter like the lady in the picture, and we'll live in a little cottage with our dog and our cat.'

'That's a lovely dream. I'd like that too – but I have to find my mama first. I know I'll get to meet her one day.'

'I know you will too, Hetty,' said Ida.

'And meanwhile you're a kind of mother to me, Ida. I know! You're my fairy godmother!' I declared.

She gave me a big hug, seemingly very moved, and then I pattered back down the stairs and hopped into my own bed in the dormitory. The sheets were icy cold, but I was still warm from the tea and Ida's hug and I went to sleep almost instantly.

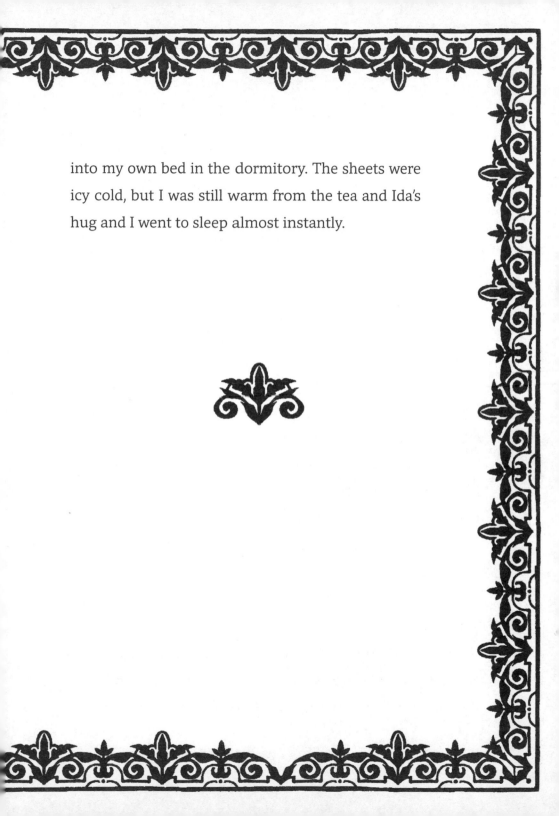

A SNOWY *Night*

FROM

THE SNOWMAN

WRITTEN BY MICHAEL MORPURGO

Illustrated by Robin Shaw

Inspired by the original tale by

RAYMOND BRIGGS

James often found that, if he pretended hard enough and squeezed his eyes tight shut, he could really make things happen. So now, because for Christmas he wanted a mountain bike with big fat tyres – a bright green one like Paul Millard had – he knew he had to pretend to go to sleep like a good little boy, as Mum had told him.

James liked Paul Millard. He had always wanted to be best friends with him. James didn't have a best friend – and he knew why. James stuttered and stammered. He always did whenever he opened his mouth and tried to speak. So at school it was better not to speak, not if he could help it. It was all right at home. For a start, he didn't stammer and stutter so much at home – and anyway, Mum and Dad never teased him. Open his mouth at school, and someone was sure to snigger or mimic him or laugh out loud. He kept quiet; kept himself to himself. It's not easy to make friends if you do that. So James spent most of the time on his own. And that made him sad.

He tried not to think about that. He thought about Paul Millard's bright green mountain bike with big fat tyres instead. It made him happier. James pretended as hard as he could to go to sleep like a good little boy. He really wanted Father Christmas to come and bring him that bike. He

pretended so well that he soon pretended himself fast asleep.

James didn't know it, but outside, as he slept, the snow did begin to fall, silently, silently – on the garden, on the duck pond, on his swing and on his trampoline, on the fields and the hedges and the trees, down on the river and up on the moor. All night the snow came floating down. All night he slept.

The moment James opened his eyes he knew the world was different, but at first he couldn't work out why. He sat up and looked out of the window. It wasn't day. It wasn't night. If it was morning already, it wasn't a morning like any other. The stars and moon were still up there, so it must still be night, but it was as bright as day. Snow! It had snowed!

Silence lay like a blanket over the house, over the farm.

And everywhere it was white. The roof of his dad's shed was white; the seat of the swing, Mum's vegetable garden, Dad's tractor – which he must have forgotten to put away again – were white. All the barns and fields and trees, the distant moors under the moon, all was silent and white.

James was still half asleep and muddle-headed, so it was a few moments before he could take it all in, and a few more before he could even begin to believe his eyes. It looked like snow, but no snow was falling. Could it really be snow? Was this a dream?

There was only one way to find out. He pulled on some clothes over his pyjamas – his trousers and the thick red jumper his mum had put out for him; the one he always wore at Christmas.

Not wanting to wake anyone – he knew he was up too early and that they would send him back to bed if they caught him – he tiptoed out of his bedroom and down the stairs, which seemed to creak more loudly than they had ever creaked before. By the back door he put on his wellies.

Bertie wanted to come with him. He sat there in his basket looking up at

him, head on one side, begging to be let out. Any moment now he would start squeaking and whining and then barking.

James crouched down. 'All right, B-Bertie,' he whispered. 'B-but if you c-come with me, not a sound, right? P-promise?'

Bertie licked his lips. It wasn't exactly a promise, James thought, but it was as good as he was going to get.

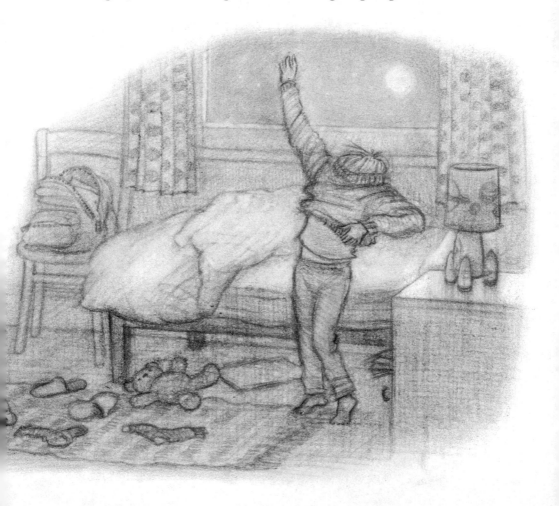

THE BAD
Dream Machine

WRITTEN BY STRUAN MURRAY

Illustrated by Manuel Šumberac

The first I knew of Wee Douglas's bad dream machine
was the mousy squeak of its wheels.

It was a beaten metal box, like a tin for sweeties
with the colour scraped off. It had two rubber wheels and a
long rope that Wee Douglas used to lead it around
like a dog.

'What's it do?' they asked on the playground.

'It takes away your bad dreams. You'll never
have them again. I got it from a witch.'

I sat with Lachlan on the steps nearby.

He'd been drawing a demon dog with fiery eyes, but he'd got distracted by the crowd round Wee Douglas.

I pulled the drawing closer to me. 'That's horrible,' I said, disgusted but also secretly impressed.

Lachlan looked at me. His eyes were all puffy, like he'd just been told off. 'It was chasing me in my dreams.' His voice dropped to a whisper. 'Melody, d'you think that machine works?'

'Course not! Wee Douglas wears his pyjamas to school.'

'You give me five pounds,' Wee Douglas was telling his audience. 'Then tap your head on the machine, and the bad dreams get sucked inside.'

The crowd laughed, but Callum Reid, whose parents gave him more pocket money than wisdom, hopped forward, waggling a fiver above his head. He got down on his knees and bonked his head on the box.

Lachlan pulled a crumpled fiver from his pocket. 'There's some chewing gum on this, d'you think he'll still take it?'

'You're saving for a phone, don't be stupid,' I said.

'But my dreams have been *really* bad lately.' Lachlan pointed to the demon dog, its toothy mouth trailing drool.

I scowled and shouted at Wee Douglas, 'If it really works, why are you charging a fiver? Do you *want* us to have bad dreams?'

Wee Douglas folded his arms. 'It's just good business,' he said loftily.

The bell rang, and everyone lined up at the door.

'You coming, Callum?' I said, noticing him still out on the playground, staring at a cloud and looking confused, like it was a flying saucer.

'Hm? Oh . . . oh aye, I'm coming.'

The next day I came into class later than everyone else and sat down. Ms Arshad wasn't here yet but the classroom was quiet. Lachlan was staring at a blank piece of paper.

'No drawings today, Lachlan?' I said.

'Don't feel like drawing.'

''S not like you,' I said, unpacking my pencil case, then letting out a big yawn that made my bones shake. I saw Wee Douglas across from me. He was playing on a fancy phone I hadn't seen him with before.

'Where'd he get that?' I said aloud. I looked around the

desks – lots of kids were staring ahead, like there was not even a single thought wandering through their minds. Smart Martha was gazing at the troll doll that hung on a key chain from her desk, like she'd forgotten why she put it there. Sad Hector had found a dead wasp on the windowsill. Normally this would have made him cry, but today he just stared and scratched his head.

I stood up. 'Hold on – did you *all* give him your money?'

Wee Douglas kept swiping his phone.

'You should pay him, Melody,' Lachlan said. 'You'll feel much better.'

'All right,' I said, narrowing my eyes at him. 'I'll make you a deal. Prove you can draw me a picture, and I'll pay him.'

Lachlan blinked. 'Don't feel like drawing.'

I got up, passing Ms Arshad on the way out of the classroom. 'Going to the loo, Ms.'

I went into the cloakroom, nudging rucksacks aside till I found it: the little beaten box with its rubber wheels. I tried to flip the lid but it was padlocked shut.

Something dropped with a jangle at my side.

'You'll need that,' said Wee Douglas. He was leaning

against the wall, eyes still on his phone.

I picked up the key.

'I'd be careful, though,' Wee Douglas said. 'All the bad dreams are in there.'

My stomach turned cold as I looked at the box. I swallowed. 'I know. But I think bad dreams might be important. The others aren't right without them.'

'Yeah, but all their worst nightmares are in that box, so . . . what do you think will happen when you open it?'

I took a deep breath, put the key in the padlock, and undid it. The padlock hit the ground with a *thunk*. I stared, listening to the pounding of my heartbeat.

I opened the box.

My big dream is to be a worldwide vet so I can save every species of animal in the whole world. Imagine a time when no trees get cut down, imagine a world where oxygen is attached to it, where every animal has a home to live in: well, this is that time. The more monkeys that have bananas, the more excellent they will feel. If guinea pigs have all the vegetables they need, then they will be delighted. Come along with me to save the world from dying out and to save the population of every animal. Follow me through the Amazon rainforest to give homes to animals who don't have homes.

So what do you say, partner? Will you come along with me on this fabulous, magical, amazing journey?

**KIERAN, AGE 10,
ST OSWALD'S CE VA PRIMARY SCHOOL**

Sweet Dreams

WRITTEN BY ANNE FINE
Illustrated by Rachael Dean

They say the same thing every night. They watch me clean my teeth. They tuck me into bed and read me my stories. Then they lean over and kiss me and they say it.

Every single time.

'Night, night. Sweet dreams.'

Sweet dreams! They're not the sort I want. Do they expect me to dream about soppy baby rabbits lolloping about in a buttercup field? Or dream about pretty little kittens?

I want to dream bigger than that. The dreams I want have thrills and dangers in them. Bright, brilliant colours. Loads of exciting things happening. I want to dream about being a firefighter at the very top of the extending ladder. The flames are rising higher. My face guard is starting to melt in the heat.

But only I am close
enough to reach out
and save the little boy,
and swing him safely
round on to the platform
beside me, then press the
button that folds the
ladder steadily down,
down to the ground,
where I hand him back
to his grateful mother
and father while everyone
else stands around cheering.

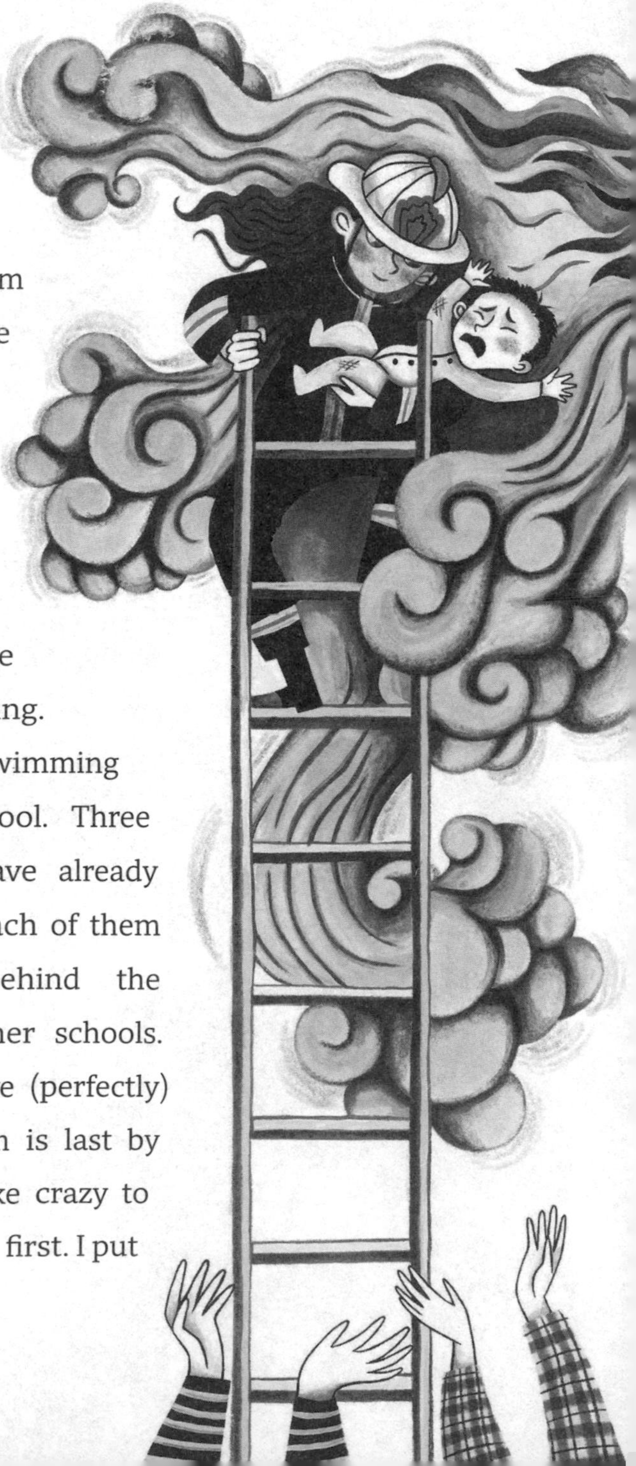

Or winning the swimming
relay race for my school. Three
people in our team have already
swum before me, and each of them
has fallen further behind the
swimmers from the other schools.
Even before I get to dive (perfectly)
into the water, our team is last by
miles. I have to swim like crazy to
catch up and overtake the first. I put

on even more of a spurt to overtake the next two, who are level pegging.

And now I only have half a length of the pool to catch up with the swimmer in front.

Can I do it?

Yes! The winner! (Well, our team, of course. But it was really me.)

Or escaping from the wizard.

I can't remember how he captured me in the first place. (That was another dream.) But I've been in his house for long enough, mopping the floors, washing the windows, chopping up stuff for his spells. I'm going to set a trap. I'll very quietly balance a bucket of icy water up over the door he leaves half open so he can spy on me, and when he comes through to tell me what to do next, the bucket will fall on his head and knock him to the floor.

That's when I'll pounce. I'll throw the dirty old rug I sleep on over his face. There's so much dust in it that he'll be half blind for a minute or two. I'll snatch his bunch of keys, unlock the cottage door and rush out, locking him in behind me. Then I'll run deep enough into the forest for him not to hear or see me when I climb up a tree with a cosy forked branch to sit in comfortably, and have the sense to wait.

The wizard will come looking, of course. He'll search for hours and hours. By the time he gives up and goes back to his cottage, it'll be dark and I'll be sleepy.

Very sleepy . . .

Very, very sleepy . . .

Fast asleep.

In the morning they ask me, as they always do, 'Sweet dreams?'

There's absolutely no point in trying to explain. It would take ages and they wouldn't be listening anyhow. It's too much of a rush in the mornings.

So I just look up from my toast and jam and say, 'Oh, yes. I dreamed of baby rabbits in a buttercup field. And pretty kittens.'

'That's nice,' they say.

And I smile and go on with my breakfast.

Waiting for Christmas

FROM

ROLL OF THUNDER, HEAR MY CRY

WRITTEN BY MILDRED D. TAYLOR

Illustrated by Chaaya Prabhat

The last days of school before Christmas seemed interminable. Each night I fell asleep with the hope that the morning would bring Papa, and each morning when he wasn't there I trudged to school consoling myself that he would be home when I returned. But the days passed, prickly cold and windy, and he did not come.

Added to the misery of the waiting and the cold was Lillian Jean, who managed to flounce past me with a superior smirk twice that week. I had already decided that she had had two flounces too many, but since I hadn't yet decided how to handle the matter, I postponed doing anything until after I had had a chance to talk with Papa about the whole Strawberry business. I knew perfectly well that he would not tear out of the house after Mr Simms as Uncle Hammer had done, for he always took time to think through any move he made, but he would certainly advise me on how to handle Lillian Jean.

Then too there was T.J., who, although not really my problem, was so obnoxiously flaunting Stacey's wool coat during these cold days that I had just about decided to deflate him at the same time I took care of Lillian Jean. Ever since the night Mr Avery had brought him to the house to return the coat and he had been told by Uncle Hammer and a faltering Stacey that the coat was his, T.J. had been more unbearable than usual. He now praised the coat from the wide tips of its lapels to the very edges of its deep hem. No one had ever had a finer coat; no one had ever looked better in such a coat; no one could ever hope to have such a coat again.

Stacey was restrained from plugging T.J.'s mouth by Uncle Hammer's principle that a man did not blame others for his own stupidity; he learned from his mistake and became stronger for it. I, however, was not so restrained and as far as I was concerned, if T.J. kept up with this coat business, he could just hit the dirt at the same time as 'Miss' Lillian Jean.

The day before Christmas I awoke to the soft murmuring of quiet voices gathered in the midnight blackness of morning.

Big Ma was not beside me, and without a moment's doubt I knew why she was gone. Jumping from the bed, my feet barely hitting the deerskin rug, I rushed into Mama's room.

'Oh, Papa!' I cried. 'I knew it was you!'

'Ah, there's my Cassie girl!' Papa laughed, standing to catch me as I leaped into his arms.

By the dawn, the house smelled of Sunday: chicken frying, bacon sizzling, and smoke sausages baking. By evening, it reeked of Christmas. In the kitchen sweet-potato pies, egg-custard pies, and rich butter pound cakes cooled; a gigantic coon which Mr Morrison, Uncle Hammer, and Stacey had secured in a night's hunt baked in a sea of onions, garlic, and

fat orange-yellow yams; and a choice sugar-cured ham brought from the smokehouse awaited its turn in the oven. In the heart of the house, where we had gathered after supper, freshly cut branches of long-needled pines lay over the fireplace mantle adorned by winding vines of winter holly and bright red Christmas berries. And in the fireplace itself, in a black pan set on a high wire rack, peanuts roasted over the hickory fire as the waning light of day swiftly deepened into a fine velvet night speckled with white forerunners of a coming snow, and the warm sound of husky voices and rising laughter mingled in tales of sorrow and happiness of days past but not forgotten.

Neet AND THE Inventor

WRITTEN BY TAMZIN MERCHANT
Illustrated by Wazza Pink

K ip's house was at the end of the street. There was only forest beyond.

The bus left a trail of dust as it trundled away. It also left a child called Neet standing in the road. It left dust and Neet and a small cardboard suitcase, to be quite precise. The suitcase contained everything Neet owned, with a generous amount of room to spare.

Before the dust had settled, someone threw open the door of the house and bounded down the garden path. The person was more a whirl of limbs and rumpled hair and enthusiasm than a sensible human shape.

'Kip?' Neet trembled a question, clutching the suitcase.

'Neet!' the whirl cried back in answer.

Neet was relieved to see kind eyes shining down as the whirl of a person came skidding to a stop.

'I'm so glad you've arrived.' Kip beamed, arms wide in welcome.

Neet coughed and stuck out a hand solemnly. Kip took it. Neet being a child and Kip being a grown-up, there was a considerable difference in height between them. But, as they shook hands, Neet felt a little bit taller.

'Can I take your suitcase?' Kip asked.

Neet clutched the suitcase closer. 'No, thank you. It contains all my things in the world. I'll hold on to it.'

Kip smiled. 'Very sensible! Bring it on in!'

Inside the house it smelled of books and beeswax and hot, delicious food. Hunger and hope flicked like shadow and light across Neet's face.

'Supper right away, I think!' Kip announced.

In the kitchen there was a big wooden table with a place laid ready. Kip pulled out a chair for Neet and bustled about, stirring a bubbling saucepan. Neet held on to the suitcase all through supper. It made eating a little awkward, but she managed.

The stew was delicious. Kip dished seconds into the bowl and Neet ate all of it. But before Kip could offer a third helping,

Neet tried unsuccessfully to stifle an enormous yawn.

'Ah. Bedtime,' Kip said decisively.

Neet (carrying the suitcase) followed Kip up the stairs. Kip showed her into a cosy room, high in the house, with smooth wooden floorboards and a little bed beneath the window. The bed had a brass frame and a neat blanket and a plump pillow.

'This is your room.' Kip smiled.

'I've never had my own room before,' Neet whispered. 'Because I . . . I'm . . .'

Neet's voice got smaller and smaller and Kip had to lean down to hear the last word, breathed low.

'You are not unwanted, Neet,' Kip replied gently. '*I* want you here, for a start. Do you hear that whispering? That's the trees saying they want you here. And see? The moon wants you too.'

The trees swayed outside. The moon beamed brightly at Neet from the sky.

'When the sun gets up in the morning, the sun will also be glad you're here,' Kip added. 'And all the birds will sing to you. Now, are you ready to hop into bed?'

Neet hesitated before confessing: 'I – I'm afraid of having bad dreams.'

'Well then!' Kip smiled. 'It's lucky that I'm an inventor.'

'An inventor?'

'Yes! And you happen to be looking at my grandest invention,' Kip announced. 'My Dream Machine.'

'Is it under the bed?' Neet asked, trying to peer beneath it while still tightly clutching the suitcase.

'Not exactly. You see, this is no ordinary bed.'

The bed looked ordinary to Neet, but Kip swept a hand proudly at it, as though it were a spaceship or a racing car.

'It took me years to perfect the Dream Machine!' Kip grinned. 'See the blanket? It's woven out of moonbeams, to soothe you to sleep. And the pillow is stuffed with night clouds, which I collected in a net. But the bed frame is my cleverest invention, if I say so myself!'

Neet squinted at the bed frame. Its brass gleamed in the lamplight.

'It's a cosmic creation that connects you to the whole universe,' Kip explained. 'When you sleep, it channels all the starlight and all the moonlight down around you, and they mingle with your sleeping mind and help you weave stories and adventures as you dream.'

Neet gazed in wonder at the Dream Machine.

'When you wake in the morning, you'll be inspired by all the adventures you've dreamed up,' Kip whispered. 'And you'll realize how many amazing things you can do out there in the world. Even though right now you feel very small and the world feels huge.'

Neet took a deep breath and walked across the room.

Kip watched as the child carefully put the suitcase down on the floor and opened it. Inside was a toothbrush, a slightly blurry photograph and a large, old-fashioned key that had once been silver but was now darkened with age.

Neet held the key tightly in both hands, eyes squeezed shut.

After a long moment she slipped the key under the pillow and gently propped the photograph on the windowsill.

'We'll be safe here,' Neet whispered to the person in the photograph.

'You will.' Kip nodded. 'I promise.'

Neet climbed into bed. The pillow was wonderfully soft.

'Goodnight, Neet,' Kip murmured. 'Sleep well. Dream beautiful dreams.'

'I will,' Neet breathed, snuggling into the blankets.

The Dream Machine glowed as Neet's eyes closed, already half dreaming.

Kip smiled and turned off the light.

When I was 7¾, I was just starting to compete in skating and surfing. I also got to travel and see other parts of the world. I knew at the time that my dream was to inspire kids around the globe to get out there and do what they love. I'm 11 now and I can't even count how many countries I've travelled to, both for competition and to skate with kids in their communities. I've taught girls all over the world how to skate. I want to continue to travel and show girls that they can do anything.

**SKY BROWN, SKATEBOARDER AND SURFER
GREAT BRITAIN'S YOUNGEST SUMMER OLYMPIAN**

THE *Lion* IN THE *Wardrobe*

WRITTEN BY SUSIE DAY
Illustrated by Lauren Beard

Jayde Jones was special.

She had the longest hair in her whole class, by seven centimetres. She had two mums: a Welsh one called Mummy, and a French one called Maman. And she was definitely the only person she knew who had a lion living in her wardrobe.

'You don't, pickle,' said Mummy, laying out Jayde's pyjamas. 'It was just a dream.'

'There's a story, isn't there, with a lion, and a wardrobe, hmm?' said Maman, as she tucked Jayde into bed. 'That's what you're thinking of. Just a story.'

But it wasn't a story. It was a lion. In her wardrobe.

And now she was in bed.

In the dark.

With a lion.

Tap tap scrabble went the lion's claws on the wooden wardrobe floor. *Slap slap thump* went the lion's lazy tail on the wooden wardrobe door. *Smack smick slurp* went the lion's lips as he licked his teeth hungrily.

My mums are rubbish, thought Jayde. *I should probably phone the police.*

But instead she got out of bed – edging carefully past the wardrobe door – and ran down the landing to Mummy and Maman's bedroom.

'I will just sleep here tonight,' said Jayde, and climbed into the warm space between them.

The next night Mummy held the wardrobe door open while Jayde got into her pyjamas. 'Look: no lion,' she said firmly.

Jayde sighed. 'That's because it's only *nearly* bedtime, Mummy. Lions only come in the deepest darkest night.'

'Maybe you need to read fewer stories, hmm?' said Maman, tucking her in.

But it wasn't a story once the lights were off.

Tap tap scrabble. Slap slap thump. Smack smick slurp.

Jayde ran down the landing again. 'I am just sleeping here again, for reasons,' she said, and tucked herself in.

The next night, while Maman found pyjamas, Mummy plugged in a new lamp. It had a soft light that cast twinkling stars all over Jayde's ceiling.

'I borrowed a book from the library,' Mummy explained. 'It's called *How to Help Girls Called Jayde Get to Sleep in Their Own Beds, Like a Grown-Up.*'

'Does it have a chapter about lions?' she asked.

'No,' said Mummy very firmly.

Jayde lay down to sleep.

She watched the twinkling stars.

Tap tap scrabble. Slap slap thump. Smack smick slurp.

'I'm hardly here at all, shh,' she said, sliding into Mummy and Maman's bed down near their feet.

The next night Mummy turned off the TV in the middle of Maman's favourite show about people baking cakes. 'No screens before bed!'

Mummy tried extra blankets, and no blankets, and hot lavender baths. She tried early bedtimes, and late ones, and all three of them running round the kitchen in the dark to get really, really tired. But none of it changed the fact that there was – still – a lion in the wardrobe.

Tap tap scrabble. Slap slap thump. Smack smick slurp.

'I give up!' shouted Mummy when Jayde climbed into their bed again. 'Three people is too many for a bed! I'm going to sleep on the sofa!'

Everyone was quite awake after that, so Maman sat up in

bed and switched on her lamp. She looked at Jayde quite seriously.

'I'm going to ask you an important question now. Jayde: is there really a lion in your wardrobe, hmm?'

Jayde nodded.

Maman patted the pile of books on her bedside table. 'OK. I took a book out of the library too – and it says lions only wake up at night-time if they're hungry. Come on.'

They both hopped out of bed. Jayde followed Maman to the kitchen, where she made hot buttered toast.

'Lions love hot buttered toast,' she explained.

They left the toast just outside the wardrobe, for the lion to fetch when it was ready. Then Maman tucked Jayde up in her own bed, and left a kiss on her pillow for later.

The next morning Jayde rushed into the kitchen with the empty plate.

'It's gone! The toast!' she said.

'So it has,' said Maman.

'And you slept in your own bed, all night!' said Mummy. 'Well, very nearly. Well done, sweetie.'

Jayde hadn't done anything at all except fall asleep. But she felt proud all over anyway.

'Do you think we should leave toast for the lion again tonight?' asked Jayde, as Maman made breakfast for all three of them: crunchy flakes for Jayde, muesli for Mummy, and hot buttered toast for Maman.

'Oh, yes,' said Maman. 'Just in case.'

Bedtime in Summer

FROM

THE BIG ALFIE AND ANNIE ROSE STORYBOOK

Written and illustrated by
SHIRLEY HUGHES

Lying in bed,

not a bit sleepy,

listening to lots of things

going on outside.

People chatting,

and watering their gardens,

and mowing the grass.

Birds calling,

boys shouting,

music from open windows

and a smell of supper.

The sun's still up.

It's slanting under the curtains.

Alfie wonders

if he went downstairs

whether they'd let him stay up, too,

just for a little while.

My big dream is to be a storywriter for all the children around the world. To take them on a journey of anything they want to see or be, and if they really believe, the characters will pop out from the book to go on the journey with them. It could be their best friend or their pet or someone from the past, but only if they let their imagination take them there!

They could battle snakes in the desert, be a grave robber from Egypt, have an adventure in a time-travelling machine to see what happens in the future, or be a SUPERHERO TO SAVE THE WORLD!!!

I want to share my love of reading with other children so I can create a whole new world with just words. It could be fantasy, love, horror or just normal everyday things. But only if they believe in the words.

ANTHONY, AGE 10, INGS FARM PRIMARY SCHOOL

⁕ Acknowledgements ⁕

Contribution copyright © Al Rodin, Aleksei Bitskoff, Alexis Deacon, Alexis Snell, Amy Sparkes, Anna Doherty, Anne Fine, Areeba Siddique, Ashley McCarthy, Ayesha L. Rubio, Beccy Speight, Ben Lerwill, Beth Lincoln, Cathy Cassidy, Charlie Higson, Chaaya Prabhat, Chris Wormell, David Roberts, Diane Ewen, Ed Vere, Eileen Kai Hing Kwan, Elisa Paganelli, Emily Sutton, Fred Blunt, Gareth Peter, Garry Parsons, Good Wives and Warriors, Hana Tooke, Henry White, Humza Arshad, Jacqueline Wilson, Jamie Littler, Jeff Kinney, Jeremy Strong, John Boyne, Katie Hickey, Kristina Stephenson, Lauren Beard, Lauren O'Hara, Lesley Barnes, Lisette Auton, Maggie Aderin-Pocock, Malorie Blackman, Manuel Šumberac, Margaux Carpentier, Maria Kuzniar, Megan Rix, Michael Rosen, Mini Grey, Mouni Feddag, Nadia Shireen, Natalia O'Hara, Nathan Bryon, Nazneen Ahmed, Nick Sharratt, Nikki Lilly, Nicola Slater, Patricia Forde, Poonam Mistry, Rachael Saunders, Rachael Dean, Rachel Morrisroe, Rashmi Sirdeshpande, Renia Metallinou, Robin Stevens, Sabrina Cohen-Hatton, Sally Anderson, Sam Copeland, Sarah Horne, Selom Sunu, Shane DeVries, Shaw Davidson, Sky Brown, Sophy Henn, Soufeina Hamed, Steven Lenton, Struan Murray, Stuart Heritage, Susie Day, Tamzin Merchant, Tom Fletcher, Wazza Pink, Yassmin Abdel-Magied 2020.

The publishers wish to thank the following for permission to reproduce copyright material. Every effort has been made to trace copyright holders. The publishers would be happy to hear from any copyright holder that has not been acknowledged.

'A Necklace of Raindrops' from *A Necklace of Raindrops and Other Stories* by Joan Aiken, illustrated by Jan Pieńkowski, published by Jonathan Cape 1968, text copyright © Joan Aiken 1968, illustrations copyright © Jan Pieńkowski 1968, reprinted by permission of The Random House Group Ltd; 'Do A Project' from *Please Mrs Butler* by Allan Ahlberg, illustrated by Fritz Wegner, published by Kestrel 1983, text copyright © Allan Ahlberg 1983, illustrations copyright © Fritz Wegner 1983, reprinted by permission of Penguin Random House; 'Self-Portrait with Butterfly' by Eric Carle, copyright © Eric Carle 1988, reprinted by permission of Eric Carle LLC; 'The Special Pumpkin' from *Tales of the Caribbean* by Trish Cooke, published by Puffin Books 2017, text copyright © Trish Cooke 2017, reprinted by permission of Penguin Random House; extract from *The Dark is Rising* by Susan Cooper, illustrated by Joe McLaren, published by Puffin Books 1976, text copyright © Susan Cooper 1973, reprinted by permission of The Random House Group Ltd copyright; extract from *The BFG* by Roald Dahl, illustrated by Quentin Blake, published by Puffin Books 1984, text copyright © The Roald Dahl Story Company Ltd 1982, illustrations copyright © Quentin Blake 1982, reprinted by permission of the Roald Dahl Story Company Ltd/Quentin Blake; 'The Giant Jumperee' by Julia Donaldson, illustrated by Helen Oxenbury, adapted from *The Giant Jumperee*, published by Puffin Books 1997, text copyright © Julia Donaldson 2020, illustration copyright © Helen Oxenbury 2020, included by permission of the author and illustrator; extract from *The Diary of a Young Girl: the Definitive Edition* by Anne Frank, edited by Otto H. Frank and Mirjam Pressler, translated by Susan Massotty, illustrated by Harry Brockway, published by Puffin Books 1997, text copyright © The Anne Frank-Fonds, Basle, Switzerland 1991, English translation copyright © Doubleday 1995, illustrations copyright © Harry Brockway 1998, text reprinted by permission of The Anne Frank-Fonds, Basle, Switzerland; 'Bedtime in Summer' from *The Big Alfie and Annie Rose Storybook* by Shirley Hughes, published by The Bodley Head 1988, copyright © Shirley Hughes 1988, reprinted by permission of The Random House Group Ltd; extract from *Stig of the Dump* by Clive King,

With thanks to Kelly Hurst, Katy Finch, Andrea MacDonald, Asmaa Isse, Helen Levene, Stephanie Barrett, Sophia Watts, Becky Chilcott, Janene Spencer, Kim Musselle, Mandy Norman and Michelle Olvera.

THANK YOU!

This book would not have been possible without the wildly imaginative support of our Puffin Big Dreamer authors and illustrators, who gave their time and creativity for a nominal fee. This generosity means that we are able to help the National Literacy Trust continue their life-changing work delivering programmes around the country.

A heartfelt thank you to all our contributors for giving your dreams to this book. Puffin would be nuffin without you!

Puffin would also like to thank the children attending schools participating in the Puffin World of Stories programme who wrote such amazing big dreams, and our Puffin supporters who told us about the wonderful dreams that inspired them as children.

The Puffin Book of Big Dreams started as a big dream of the team at Puffin to celebrate Puffin's 80th birthday. We hope you have enjoyed reading it. Dream big, read Puffin.